WHALE HARBOR HORIZONS

SALTWATER SUNSETS BOOK FOUR

FIONA BAKER

Published in the United States of America

First Edition, 2023

fionabakerauthor.com

JOIN MY NEWSLETTER

If you love beachy, feel-good women's fiction, sign up to receive my newsletter, where you'll get free books, exclusive bonus content, and info on my new releases and sales!

Whale Harbor and its people. As she pushed the returns cart from one row to the next, its one squeaky wheel joined the rest of the buzz of life. It was peaceful, in a way, even if it wasn't quiet.

Despite that, her attention was drawn toward her phone for what had to be the sixth time in the last half an hour, as she pulled it from her pocket just enough to check the time. In theory, her shift had also ended half an hour ago, but she was waiting for a call. The idea of just pacing her kitchen while she waited seemed unbearable though, so she had taken the excuse to get some reshelving done.

She was supposed to have FaceTimed Connor during her lunch break, but it had still been early for him, and he'd had to cancel the call. Apparently, there had been a meeting as soon as he got to work that day, and it had caught him off guard. He had promised to call her that evening though. He hadn't been specific on the time, saying he'd try to call around "three-ish" his time or around six her time, so that just left Monica waiting.

She tried not to consider it *sad* that she had to schedule FaceTime dates with her boyfriend, and even then they tended to get canceled. After all, Connor wasn't doing it on purpose. He was just

CHAPTER ONE

At six-thirty in the evening, the Whale Harbor Public Library was still buzzing with activity, even on a Tuesday. Despite the stereotypes, it was not a quiet building. Keyboards clicked and clacked. Books thumped and pages shuffled. The kids section was playing host to a crafting class for kids whose parents worked late. One of the conference rooms held an ESL lesson and another was hosting a sign language class for people who couldn't attend classes earlier in the day.

It was not a particularly quiet building, despite the stereotypes, but Monica Grey would never want it to be. She loved seeing all the life was around her and knowing how much the library was doing for working as hard as he could to get his business off the ground.

Besides, it had been weeks since they had seen each other in person, and it had been nearly as long since they had had more than a brief phone call or a distracted series of texts. Monica would take what she could get. And wasn't that a thought? Once upon a time, she dreamed of starting a bed and breakfast with cozy reading nooks and a reading room, where she could lead beach walks on the weekend. Now, she dreamed of a day when Connor Burke could make more than a few minutes for her.

She pushed that thought out of her mind, adjusting her glasses on the bridge of her nose. She wasn't being fair, and she knew it. Connor always sounded so excited whenever he talked about moving to Whale Harbor and working remotely, just as soon as he got the business established. Monica knew he loved her and that he was doing his best to be with her. It was just taking longer than anticipated.

The first time she had seen Connor off at the airport, two years ago, this hadn't been where she had seen their relationship going.

Her phone rang at last, interrupting the gloomy thought. It was nearly seven o'clock by now, and the library was nearly empty, but Monica started hurrying toward the main entrance regardless. Taking a phone call in the library just seemed tacky, even if it was just a phone call and not the FaceTime Connor had promised.

She barely managed a brief, "Hey," when she answered the phone before Connor started talking.

"I know you're going to be upset," he began quickly, not even saying hello. "But I won't be able to make the flight out there next week. I'll make it up to you. Scout's honor."

Monica could feel her heart sinking toward her stomach.

"So, what?" she asked, twisting a lock of her blonde hair around her finger. "Are you going to be a day or two late?"

The other end of the line was quiet for a moment, in the way it usually was when Connor was picking his words. Monica knew what he was going to say before he actually said it. Dread settled in her chest before following her heart downward. For as much as Connor had talked about them starting that B&B together once they were living on the same coast, she wondered if he would ever make it a priority.

Finally, Connor cleared his throat, the sound rendered into static through the phone. "The logistics just aren't going to work out," he settled on carefully. "It's for the best if we just reschedule the entire trip for some time when there's less going on."

"Oh," Monica mumbled, her voice low and flat. She didn't remind him that he always had something going on. Over the last two years, they had seen each other so little. He had to be aware of that. He didn't need her to remind him or start hanging it over his shoulders like some sort of albatross.

"I'll make it up to you," Connor repeated quickly, and he sounded so earnest. He really did mean to make it up to her. "First chance I get to come out there, we'll do whatever you want. I promise."

"It's okay," Monica offered quietly. Even though she didn't want Connor to feel bad, she couldn't manage to make her voice sound cheerful. The disappointment felt heavy on her shoulders. "We'll make it work eventually."

"I knew you would understand." There was another burst of static as Connor sighed in relief. "I'll talk to you again soon."

Monica didn't even get to say goodbye before the line went dead. She stood on the sidewalk in front of the library for a moment, staring at her phone in her hand, as if she could simply will Connor into calling her back and for an actual conversation.

She shoved her phone back into her pocket. It was still the middle of the afternoon in San Francisco, she reminded herself. Connor was still in the middle of his work day. He would have more to say that evening. Monica would just have to call him or text him after dinner. She let that thought fall over her as something almost like comfort as she headed for her car to head home.

It was quiet on Friday save for the sound of the water lapping against the hull of the ship and the gulls crying above. At one point in time, Braden Watson would never have dreamed of needing to wake up at four o'clock in the morning. The ocean never slept though, so there was no time to waste.

It was peaceful on the boat, although not too long ago he never would have imagined thinking so. He had dreamed of being an architect in the past, and his father had never hidden how he felt about that. Braden coming back from Washington D.C. and stepping onto the boat had initially just been a temporary measure after his father died.

It had spiraled from there. He had lengthened his stay as his relationship with his mother improved, and then again in December when a blizzard had blown through town like a wrecking ball, leaving downed power lines, broken windows, and some structural damage in its wake.

The town needed all the help they could get to fix the damage and keep everything running smoothly, and Braden had stayed to help and to work on a project the storm had also taken a toll on. And suddenly it was March, and he was out on that boat every morning at what had once seemed like an ungodly hour.

Braden chuckled to himself, scrubbing a hand through his slightly messy blond hair. There were plenty of days where four o'clock still felt too early, but he was getting used to it, slowly but surely.

The early mornings were worth it though. His relationship with his mother was better than it had been in years, and while Braden was certainly a grown man and his mother's professor boyfriend hadn't been in the picture for very long, Thomas was nevertheless a good man with a lot of advice to offer.

By five-thirty in the morning, Braden was just about ready to cast off for the morning. He untied the ship from the mooring posts and then hurried back aboard as it began to drift. The engine engaged with a churning clunk that had the entire deck rumbling, and soon enough the ship was off onto the water.

Braden's crew wasn't particularly large, but there were enough of them to get the job done, and they worked well together. Even if he occasionally had to talk some sense into the youngest members, who were just out of high school and determined to try stuffing fish guts down each other's jackets. He had mentioned them to his mother once, and she hadn't been surprised to hear about their antics. Gabrielle Watson never forgot a student, and they had been just as rowdy when they had been in her class.

Some days were rougher than others, depending on the weather, and some catches were more impressive than others. By the time the ship was docked once again that afternoon, it had been a calm day and while the catch was nothing record breaking, it was respectable all the same.

It was early in the afternoon as the crew readied to disembark—one of the perks of starting so early in the morning—so it was no surprise that there were people on the docks. It was around lunchtime, and the marina was a popular place for people to take their breaks because of its beauty, even if the weather in March was still pretty chilly.

Walter, Braden's second-hand man in the business, was in charge of making sure the day's catch got sold and transported to the places it needed to go. He had been doing it for far longer than Braden had been back in town, and Braden wasn't going to pretend he could do it better even if he had technically "taken over" his father's business. As he double-checked that Walter had everything he needed for the afternoon, Braden caught sight of a familiar figure out of the corner of his eye.

Braden glanced over his shoulder, and there was Monica Grey, leaning on the railing of one of the docks and looking over the water. She had a look on her face like her thoughts had suddenly stalled out after racing halfway around the globe and back, and Braden wondered what she was thinking so hard about.

And then she caught him staring. She cocked her head to the side and arched an eyebrow, before lifting a hand and offering him a small wave. Braden waved back, his heart picking up its pace in his chest.

He had always known Monica was gorgeous. Even after returning from D.C., when he expected everyone and everything in the small town to seem slow and dull in comparison, Monica had been a bright spot, full of light and life. Of course, it was common knowledge that Monica was in a relationship, even if Braden didn't even know what the guy looked like, so he was never going to do anything about it. Even so, his heart raced.

The moment ended as Monica checked the time on her phone and began to leave, presumably heading back to the library. Braden dragged his attention back to Walter, who was watching him with a sly, knowing smile.

"Shut up," Braden groused, grumpy but good-natured.

"I didn't say anything," Walter replied, holding his hands up in feigned surrender. "I wouldn't dream of it."

Braden rolled his eyes, but let the topic drop. "You need anything, or are you good to go?"

"Good to go," Walter confirmed, preemptively waving Braden off. "You head on home, and we'll do it all again tomorrow."

Braden waved over his shoulder as he turned to go. Eventually, 'doing it all again tomorrow' might start to seem too boring and repetitive, but he wasn't sure. He hadn't even expected to like being back in Whale Harbor to begin with. He certainly wasn't going to try making predictions about how long it would hold his interest.

Maybe he would still be there in five years. Maybe he would have moved on for something a bit faster paced within the next five months.

For the time being, he was content, so he wasn't going to stress out about it too much.

CHAPTER TWO

It was a quiet Monday afternoon at Sand 'n' Things. Marty Sims hadn't even needed to put up a sign when she ate her lunch a couple of hours ago. It was nothing out of the ordinary though. It was the awkward stage between major holidays, where people had already decorated for one season and it wasn't quite time for them to start purchasing decorations for the next season. There were a few lulls like that every year at her interior design shop, and Marty knew they were nothing to worry about.

Marty used the quiet to her advantage, standing in front of one of her window displays and mentally mapping out how she wanted to update it as spring became summer. As she pondered and planned, Peaches, her beloved orange cat, wove between her legs in figure eights, over and over, purring all the while. It was as if she had forgotten that she saw Marty all day every day and so was constantly thrilled to see her again—or maybe she was just taking advantage of being the only cat in the building. While Peaches continued to come into work with Marty, the other three cats stayed home during the day.

Marty reached down to scratch Peaches' ears as she planned her window display. The image building in Marty's head was bright and floral, with a few sprays of the long, dark green sea grasses that grew on the beaches. Something tasteful but eye-catching, and maybe even a bit more colorful than she was used to going.

Her creativity was where she felt adventurous, and she had been feeling more adventurous since Wyatt Jameson had come into her life. She had felt stagnant before he'd opened up *Wyatt's Quads* and moved back into town to stay. While his interests would never entirely be hers, he made her feel brave and adventurous. It was so freeing, compared to how every choice had once sat upon her shoulders like they were waiting for her to make the wrong one.

The bell over the door dinged cheerfully as it opened, pulling Marty from her thoughts. It was no matter though. She had time yet before she had to settle on a new display. She turned toward the door, ready to greet a customer, but instead saw Monica. Her librarian friend was wearing her usual large glasses, and her blonde hair was pulled back into a neat ponytail.

"Oh, hey!" she called cheerfully, bending to scoop Peaches up before moving to meet Monica by the door. The movement to avoid tripping over the orange cat was second nature. "What's going on?" she asked, concern already forming in her mind.

Monica looked tired, her green eyes a little hazy, and Marty knew that was unusual for her. Initially, Monica had been closer with Marty's sister Darla than with Marty, but ever since Darla had moved back into Whale Harbor, their friend groups had more or less conjoined. Marty had gotten to know Monica enough to recognize when something was wrong.

Monica sighed slowly and admitted, "Connor was supposed to be here this week, but he had to cancel. I was hoping he would just be able to catch a flight a day or two later, but I guess there was no way for him to get that to work out." Her mouth twisted to the side. "I could almost understand it, you know? I know how busy he is. But he keeps missing

FaceTime calls too, and at this point I'm not even sure what I'm still holding out for if he can't even make time to call me every so often. You know?"

Immediately, Marty knew the situation was going to need more attention than she could spare while still minding the shop. Monica had always been so sure of Connor and how they were meant for each other, or at least she had always seemed to be. Marty could only wonder how long her feelings had been bubbling under the surface for her to finally admit them.

"This sounds like a conversation that needs coffee," she declared, before grabbing her tote bag and plopping Peaches into it. "Let's go. It's on me."

"I would hate to pull you away from work," Monica tried to protest, although the effort sounded pretty halfhearted to Marty's ears.

Marty pointedly glanced around the shop, empty at the moment save for the two of them. Monica huffed, the noise caught somewhere between a sigh and a laugh, and motioned Marty along. Marty set a little sign in the window, cheerfully proclaiming '*Out for lunch!*' in loopy script, and flipped the sign on the door to '*Closed*' as they left.

Seastar Espresso was always a welcome sight, and Marty savored the smell of the coffee and tea brewing as she pushed the door open and stepped inside. Peaches poked her nose out of the tote to sniff the air, but she didn't try to escape. Cats generally weren't among the cafe's accepted clientele, but as long as Peaches didn't try to go anywhere, Marty knew that Charity Turner, the proprietor, would make an exception. It was almost a shame that it was still the middle of the school day though. Charity's son Lucas would have gotten a kick out of the tabby in the tote.

Charity waved from behind the counter as Marty and Monica entered. She was a tall, pretty woman with tan skin, jet black hair, and brown eyes that gleamed warmly as she greeted them.

"Your usual?" she asked as she rang up another customer's order. She waited for Marty and Monica to nod before waving them along to a table.

They sat down at a table toward the back of the cafe, sitting across from each other at a booth, and at first Monica didn't say anything. Marty didn't push her to talk. It seemed like she needed to gather her thoughts.

Soon enough, there was no one at the counter, and Charity approached, balancing three mugs with the ease of a lot of practice. She set them down on the table and then took a seat beside Marty. She folded an arm on the table and propped her chin up in the other hand.

"All right, what's got this table looking so gloomy?" she asked.

Charity was always willing to lend an ear when it seemed like someone needed one. It was no wonder she had blended in seamlessly to the group with Marty, Monica, and Darla.

Monica sipped her drink before letting out a long sigh. "Connor had to cancel his trip, and he usually can't even be bothered to FaceTime me anymore. And even when he does, he only has a few minutes." She stared down at her mug and traced the tip of one finger around the rim of it. "I don't know why we're still together, if he doesn't even want to talk to me anymore."

Charity's eyebrows rose in surprise, but she stayed tactfully quiet.

"I don't want to think that this isn't worth it," Monica continued after a moment, frowning down at her mug. "If it isn't worth it now, that means it wasn't ever worth it, which means I've wasted two years of my life waiting for him to throw me a few scraps. I want to believe that Connor cares about me, but I'm just..." She trailed off for before shrugging. "I'm just getting tired of waiting for him to actually *show* it, I guess."

"What are you going to do about it?" Marty asked gently.

"I'm not sure," Monica replied, but her voice was soft and small, sad in a way that had Marty thinking that Monica knew exactly what she needed to do, even if she didn't want to acknowledge it quite yet.

"Well, whatever you decide on, you know we all have your back," Charity added, reaching across the table to squeeze Monica's hand briefly. "Darla too."

"Of course," Marty agreed. "You could probably even convince her to let you throw paint all over the place for stress relief. Like one of those rage rooms on a serious budget."

"Oh, man." Monica laughed quietly. "Connor would hate that. Or... I think he would, at any rate. It feels like we barely know each other anymore, with how long we've been apart. I sort of thought that we would just snap back to normal once we were together again, but..." She trailed off, looking glum.

"But if he's never going to prioritize being with you, are you ever really going to know him?" Charity finished for her. "Honestly, it doesn't really sound like this relationship is feeding your soul at this point."

"I know, I know." Monica sighed. "It's a lot to think about, and a lot that I don't want to think about. But I know what I need to do. I think I just need to go psych myself up for a while first."

"You know where we are if you need some backup cheerleaders," Marty replied. "Just a quick phone call, and we'll be there with pompoms and everything." Granted, Marty had never been a cheerleader, but it was funny how many elements of interior décor looked a bit like pompoms. She waved her hands like she was already holding a pair, hoping it would make Monica cheer up, at least a little.

Monica smiled at her crookedly. "I know. And if it seems like I'm not making the choice I need to make, I'll be sure to call in backup. For now, I just need to mentally prep myself."

She finished her drink and set the mug down, before getting to her feet. "Thanks for listening," she offered, as she stepped away from the table.

"Anytime," Charity assured her. "You know that." The women exchanged quick hugs.

As Monica left the cafe, Marty's thoughts turned to Wyatt, and she couldn't help but to think that Monica needed someone like him. Not exactly like Wyatt, of course, but someone steady and present, and someone ready and willing to support her and be there for her. Maybe Connor could be that for someone, but it was pretty clear he couldn't be there for Monica.

* * *

The engine of the quad growled as the quad raced over the grass and stone, bouncing and jolting as it crunched branches and churned up stones with ease. For the longest time, it was not a noise Wyatt's neighbors had been accustomed to hearing on a Saturday afternoon, but he was grateful they had adjusted quickly and with minimal fuss.

The quad transitioned easily from dirt back to pavement as Wyatt steered it onto the road, and it coasted down in speed as he turned back into the drive in front of *Wyatt's Quads*, where the quad eased to a halt. Everything seemed to be working perfectly, and the newly restored little beast was sure to be a hit in the shop. It was orange and white, and it had been filthy when he'd gotten his hands on it. It had been in quite a state back then. Wyatt had taken to calling it 'Trouble,' after Marty's calico cat.

Wyatt dismounted from the quad and pulled his helmet off, shaking out his short, wavy brown hair. He set the helmet aside on the seat of the quad so he could pull his phone out of his jacket's inner pocket. He was just trying to check the time, but the cell phone chose that moment to start ringing as 'Dad' popped up on the caller ID.

He accepted the call, answering it with, "Hey, Dad. Everything good?"

"Better than good," his father replied, sounding more energized than Wyatt had heard him in quite some time. "There's an event coming up in the city, and we've been picked as the main quad shop represented!"

For a moment, all Wyatt could do was stare blankly at the quad in front of him, processing those words. After a moment, he shook his head quickly, laughing incredulously as he did. "Are you serious?"

"As a heart attack," his father assured him. "This is going to do great things for us, and I don't even know if it would have happened if we hadn't become business partners."

"Dad, come on," Wyatt huffed quietly, stuffing his free hand into his pocket.

"Take the compliment," his father ordered him wryly. "I'll call back when I've got more details."

"Sounds good. Talk to you soon."

As the line went dead, Wyatt heaved a sigh, the breath ending on another laugh as he did. Everything had been coming up aces since he moved back to Whale Harbor. It was one of the best decisions he had made for himself. That made him think about the very best part of his choice to move back: his relationship with Marty.

Rather than put his phone away, he pulled up Marty's number and called her.

"Hey!" he greeted her cheerfully once she picked up. "I'm heading home soon. I've got amazing news!"

CHAPTER THREE

Monica loved the library. It was one of her favorite places in the world, and she often spent even her days off there, browsing the shelves and then finding a comfortable chair to read it, in before finding yet another book to take to the beach later. Considering that, she almost felt guilty for how much she did not want to be there on that Monday afternoon.

She was moderately comforted by the knowledge that she didn't really want to be *anywhere* just then. Her head had been too busy, and so the entire world felt full and cramped, so even the library had started to feel a bit suffocating. And she hadn't even talked to anyone about it. She had told Marty and Charity she was going to break up with Connor after she gave herself a pep talk. She was pretty sure they weren't expecting it to take her a week to give herself a pep talk. Even if she knew they wouldn't judge her for it —she was pretty sure there was nothing she could do that would make them judge her harshly—she nevertheless didn't want to admit to anyone that she still hadn't cut that cord.

After work, she kept telling herself. She would call him and get it over with after work. She just had to put it out of her mind until then.

Ultimately, it seemed like the universe as a whole did not want to let her do that. At around one o'clock, her phone rang, and when she pulled it out of her pocket to check, she was stunned to see Connor's name. He rarely called her so early in the day. For him, it wasn't even lunch time yet. She glanced around quickly and, seeing that the section of the library she was in just then was fairly quiet, she stepped between two rows of shelves and answered the call. She supposed she could just get it over with now, instead of holding off until after work.

"Is everything all right?" she asked, concerned right out of the gate. She knew she was planning on breaking up with him, but she couldn't help that instinct.

"Yeah, yeah," he replied, sounding distracted. "It's fine. I just..." He trailed off, and a wiggling worm of dread began to inch its way up the back of Monica's throat.

Connor sighed, cleared his throat, and finally said, "I just don't think this is working. The two of us, I mean." As if he actually needed to clarify what he was talking about. Like he thought she was an idiot.

Monica felt, of all things, a thread of irritation. *She* had planned on breaking up with *him*, and now she didn't even get that much. But that certainly wasn't a helpful thought right then, so she coiled that irritation up and shoved it to the back of her thoughts.

Even so, the emotion that had been building up all week leaked out a little. Her voice was already wobbling slightly as she asked, "It took you two years to tell me that you don't want to be with me? You couldn't have ripped that bandage off any quicker?"

"It's not like that," he protested. "But I decided I'm done lying to myself. You—you're amazing, Monica. You're a great girl. But I don't want to live in Whale Harbor. It's too small and quiet. It would never give me everything I'm looking for. And you would never be happy in San Francisco. So it seemed like the better thing to do, to cut us both loose instead of forcing one of us to be miserable later on."

And just like that, Monica couldn't even say he was wrong. It felt like the final slap in the face just then.

"If you're sure," she mumbled into the phone. "I guess this is goodbye, then."

"Goodbye, Monica."

He barely even sounded disappointed as he said it, and the line went dead before Monica could get another word in. The world seemed too quiet suddenly, as she pulled her phone away from her face and stared at it, as if she could just will it into ringing again.

She didn't even realize she was crying until a tear landed on her phone screen. Hastily, she scrubbed the screen off on her shirt and put it back into her pocket, before retreating toward the main desk. At least then if any patrons were about to approach, she would be able to see them coming, instead of them taking her by surprise in her current state.

Or at least that was the idea. She was halfway back to the desk when someone cleared their throat from between two sets of shelves, and Monica whipped around to face them.

She met Braden Watson's blue eyes and immediately felt her face heat. She certainly hadn't intended to get into this state at work, and a patron catching her like this was definitely not making the situation any better. And Braden himself looked equal parts baffled and concerned, because of course he probably was. No one walked into the library and expected to find one of the librarians having an emotional breakdown.

He was holding two books in one hand, tucked against his hip. With his other hand, he pulled a packet of tissues out of his jacket pocket and offered them to her, his brow still knotted in puzzled concern. The sheer unexpectedness of the gesture and the fact that Braden looked a bit like a bewildered golden retriever finally managed to wring a small, damp laugh out of Monica, and she reached out to pull a tissue from the packet.

"Thanks," she murmured, dabbing at her face with the tissue. "Welcome to your... completely normal, run-of-the-mill public library," she offered, trying to lighten the mood. "How can I help you?"

"Uh—" Braden stammered for a moment, seeming unsure what to say before he shook his head slightly and held up the books in his hand. "My mom checked out a couple of books a few days ago, and I told her I would return them for her while I was out running errands," he explained.

He was doing an admirable job of pretending

that the situation was completely normal, but it was still pretty obvious that he was confused and concerned about everything that had just happened. He set the books down on the counter and ran a hand through his blond hair awkwardly.

"Right. Of course." Monica finished dabbing at her face, gave herself a mental shake, and made a note to go to the back room later to check on her makeup. In theory, her eyeliner and mascara were waterproof, but she wasn't sure how much faith she was willing to put into that claim just then.

She tucked the tissue into her pocket and reached out for the books as Braden slid them over to her. "No problem. I'll get these checked in for you."

She finished the short walk back to the main desk and stepped behind it, but she could hear Braden following her cautiously, as if he was waiting for her to suddenly drop to the floor and break down. Granted, she knew realistically that he wasn't waiting for anything like that to happen. He was simply a good man, and while they weren't the closest of friends, they had nevertheless had several good conversations with each other since the holiday potluck. It only made sense that he would be concerned when he had never seen her like this before.

Monica tried not to acknowledge it as she checked the books back in and set them on the returns cart parked by the desk. It took a bit longer than usual. She could feel a headache growing behind her forehead, and staring at the computer monitor just then was not her favorite activity. To make matters more awkward, not acknowledging the situation got a bit difficult when Braden finally asked, slowly and cautiously, "So, are you okay?"

Monica huffed out a quiet laugh at the absurdity of the situation, even if she didn't really think it was that funny. She pinched the bridge of her nose between two fingers for a second before letting her hand fall back down to the desk.

"I'm fine," she assured him. "It's nothing you need to worry about, but thank you."

He didn't look convinced, but Monica didn't give him the chance to start prying.

"How is Gabrielle, anyway?" she asked. "I haven't seen her in ages."

"Oh, she's fine," Braden replied, his expression lightening immediately as the topic switched to his mother. It was pretty cute, honestly, and Monica was glad to see it. She wasn't going to bring it up—it was none of her business, regardless of how far small-town gossip could spread—but she knew they hadn't always been as close as they were now. Gabrielle was a good woman who cared a lot about the town and the people in it. Monica was pretty sure she still cared about every student she had ever had as if she were their mother. She deserved to have a life full of people who cared about her.

"Good, that's good," Monica mused, half of her attention still focused on the computer in front of her. She didn't want to be actively rude, but she also didn't want to encourage Braden to stay any longer than he needed to right then. On any other day, Monica would be happy to talk to him, but just then, it was really not her day—and that wasn't even taking it into account that she was still on the clock.

Despite that, she still found herself asking, "How are the house renovations coming? I know you had some trouble with them after that storm swept through." It seemed as if everyone in town had had some sort of trouble after that catastrophe, including the library. Half of the windows in the kids' section had cracked or shattered, and the back half of the basement had been flooded with three inches of water. The cleanup had been terrible even though Monica knew they'd gotten off easily compared to a lot of folks.

"They're nearly done," he replied, and Monica

was certain she could detect a hint of pride in his voice. "Honestly, I like the work, but I won't be upset when they're fully finished, and then all I need to concentrate on is waking up before the crack of dawn."

"And how's *that* going?" Monica asked wryly. "How goes the fishing, Ahab?"

Braden rolled his eyes, but it was a good-natured gesture. "My white whale is still out there somewhere, but it's going pretty well besides that. I'm enjoying it more than I expected to."

"That's good," Monica replied, before letting the topic settle and drop.

Braden lingered for a moment longer, concern creeping back into his expression. For a second, Monica was convinced he was going to ask her if she was all right again, but he managed to wrestle the urge under control.

"I suppose I'll get out of your hair, then," he finally said, glancing down at his watch. "Try not to work too hard, all right?"

"Aye aye, Captain," she assured him, as she lifted a hand and waved him on his way.

Braden accepted it as the pleasant dismissal it was meant to be, and he turned on his heel and ambled his way back toward the main doors.

And just like that, Monica was on her own again. She stared down at the desk, her fingers drumming absentmindedly on the surface. She sort of hated that Braden had seen her like that, but at the same time, the sudden quiet wasn't any better.

She tipped her head back and dug the heels of her hands against her eyes for a moment, before heaving a sigh and letting her hands fall away. She could tough it out for a few more hours, and once she was back home, she could cry as much as she wanted to without anyone walking in on her.

CHAPTER FOUR

Whale Harbor had many things, despite being a relatively small town, but one thing it did not yet have was an art museum. Not for lack of effort though. Darla Sims was pouring her heart and soul into getting the fledgling museum she had been working at up and on its feet. It wasn't ready to open, but thanks to her own efforts and the efforts of the amazing team working with her, it had come a long way.

She didn't want to feel ungrateful for what she had, and she was proud of what she was doing. Even so, it felt as if she hadn't seen her fiancé Rick in ages. That wasn't quite true—they saw each other several times a week still—but it just wasn't the same when they were both distracted and tired. Darla was up to her elbows in errands for the museum, and now that winter was well and truly behind them for the season, Rick Maroney was busy getting the whale-watching tours up and running again while still balancing his work at the Marine Center.

They both loved what they did. Neither of them would trade their jobs. Even so, they were both tired and busier than either of them had any right to be. They had barely even made any headway on wedding plans. Every time they tried to sit down and discuss it so they could at least pick a date, something else reared its head and needed either Darla's attention or Rick's.

Darla hadn't thought getting a museum off the ground would be easy. Starting any new project was never easy, after all. Despite that, it was still proving to be more stressful than she had anticipated it would be. She couldn't regret it though. It was a culmination of basically all of her dreams, aside from the dreams that related to Rick.

She tried not to think it was unfair, how getting an art museum established meant she had hardly any time for her own art. It seemed like a very rude sort of irony, but it was also not exactly surprising.

More than anything, Darla was getting tired of playing the world's longest game of phone tag, she reflected as she frowned down at her cell phone, blowing a lock of auburn hair out of her eyes.

Between confirming a shipment of supplies and coordinating a few of the contractors, she had finally had a moment to pause and take a breath, and she wasn't even surprised to realize she had missed yet another call from Rick. And she knew she couldn't even call him back right then. He was in the middle of a shift at the Marine Center, and Darla wasn't even sure if he would have his phone on him. If he did, she knew he wasn't going to answer it while he was on the job.

She settled for firing off a quick text apologizing for missing his call—again—and letting him know she was looking forward to seeing him later, before she shoved her phone back into her purse for the time being. She needed to make one more quick check on how the museum was proceeding, and then she would be able to actually stop and take a breath.

Luckily enough, Darla was not the only one involved with the museum who knew what she was doing. For the moment, everything was going well enough, and she didn't need to put out any fires, literal or metaphorical. Rick was still at work though, so when she pulled her phone back out of her purse, she called her mother instead. She still didn't have incredibly high hopes that it would go well. Her mother was on a cruise she had gotten as a gift for Christmas, and whether or not she had any cell phone reception was a bit up in the air. Sometimes calls went through just fine. Sometimes they didn't go through at all. Most annoyingly, sometimes they went through but it was impossible to hear what she was saying.

Luck was on Darla's side for that moment though. The phone rang a few times, and then Lori Sims answered with a pleasant, "Good afternoon, dear."

Darla could pick up a breeze on the other end of the line, but other than that, she could hear perfectly fine.

"Hi, Mom."

Lori paused for a moment, then laughed. "Oh, wait. It is afternoon there, isn't it? I've never been very good at time zones."

That wasn't exactly a shocking discovery. Lori had scarcely left Whale Harbor since moving in. She had never had to contend with anything other than daylight savings time.

"You're fine," Darla assured her. "I just wanted to call and check in while I've got the time to do so."

"Still being kept busy by the museum?" Lori asked sympathetically.

"Like you wouldn't believe." Darla sighed. "But I didn't call about that right now. How are you? How's the cruise going?"

"Oh, honey, it's wonderful!" her mother gushed, and Darla tried to recall a time when she had heard her mother sound quite so excited.

"Have you met anyone?" Darla asked slyly, even if she already had a decent idea of the answer she was going to get. As far as she could tell, her mother hadn't been looking for *that* kind of company for a very long time, and it was probably going to take more than a single cruise to change that. Even so, Darla was open to the idea of it. Her mom deserved good things and good people in her life.

True to form, Lori scoffed. "Oh, don't be silly. It's nothing like that. It's just so nice to talk to people about something other than real estate and property taxes. I can go up on deck and take a walk in the sun, and I don't have to do anything. I can just appreciate the view or talk to people. It's lovely. Why, I've even realized that I like dancing!"

Darla felt a bit of tension she had hardly even noticed was there begin to unknot and relax. Her mom liked to keep busy, but she had always done so with work. It was incredible to hear that she was finding actual hobbies, finally.

"That's great!" Darla replied. "You'll have to tell me what sort of music you like later, all right?"

"Of course, dear," Lori agreed, before hurriedly adding, "But I've got to go, dear. There's a show starting soon, and I don't want to miss it."

Darla smiled to herself, regardless of the fact that her mother wasn't there right to see it. "Talk to you later, then. Have fun."

"It was lovely hearing from you!" Lori offered, before the line went dead.

Darla pulled the phone away from her face to put into her purse, but she paused when she realized she had a text from her sister. Eyebrows rising, she opened the message.

MARTY: Hey, Monica and Connor called it quits, and I don't think Monica is taking it too well. We're going to need all hands on deck.

Darla winced before she could help it, and she was glad there was no one there to see her just then. She couldn't say she was surprised to realize it had happened—she had met Connor once, only very briefly, and it had been ages ago because it seemed like getting him to visit was like pulling teeth with a spoon—but she had been *hoping* it wouldn't come to that. As farfetched as she knew it was, she had been hoping Monica would get the fairy tale she had been holding out for over the past two years. It seemed like the least Connor owed her after everything else.

Darla pushed the thought away. Relationships weren't supposed to be based on who owed what to whom, and she knew that. Besides, that was irrelevant by this point regardless. The important part was Monica, and making sure she was all right and that she knew she wasn't alone.

She had to get back to work pretty soon, so she didn't have time to call Monica just then, but she did at least have time to let Monica know that Darla was thinking of her. She wrote up a quick text and hit send.

DARLA: Hey. Marty told me about what happened. I am so sorry. If you need me for anything, you know I'll be there. Anything! Need to talk? Need me to pick up a pint of ice cream? Need help hiding the evidence? Just let me know. I've got your back.

She wasn't expecting to get a reply right then

and there, so she checked the time once again, put her phone back into her purse, and quickly got back to work. As an afterthought, she pulled her phone out of her purse to instead put it into her pocket. If she got another text, she would know about it immediately.

CHAPTER FIVE

The world never made time for anyone to just be upset, but on Tuesday evening as she was closing up the shop, Marty finally got the text from Monica that she had been expecting, and she leapt into action.

The first course of action was to drop Peaches off at home, and then to stop by *The Blue Crab* on the way to Monica's house. The restaurant hadn't been in Whale Harbor for too long—certainly nowhere near as long as *Clownfish Eatery*, where Marty worked one day a week—but they had quickly become the place to go for fancier fare or an incredible dessert. Marty picked up one of their well-loved strawberry-rhubarb pies. Dessert and a movie wouldn't fix the situation, but it would at least make it a little bit better.

When Marty pulled into Monica's driveway, she could see the lights on through the windows, but she couldn't see anyone moving around inside. She was worried, for a moment, that Monica had stepped out and Marty had missed her, until she saw a silhouette in the kitchen. Evidently, Monica hadn't even realized Marty had arrived.

With a sigh, Marty got out of the car and knocked on Monica's door. A moment later, Monica opened the door, and she was already holding a glass of wine in one hand, with the bottle tucked into the crook of her arm.

Oh boy, Marty thought to herself, eyeing the bottle for a second. *It must be worse than I thought.*

But she wasn't there to judge, and it was clear that she had come at just the right time.

She brandished the cardboard box with the pie inside at Monica. "I come bearing an offering."

"Oh, thank goodness. Pie sounds perfect right now." Monica blew out a breath, stepping aside to let Marty in. As she disappeared into the kitchen to get a second wine glass, Marty made her way into the living room. There were DVDs and Blu-rays on the TV stand, the floor, and the coffee table, as if Monica had been sorting through her entire collection to find the perfect movie for the situation.

As she glanced over the various movie titles, Marty was pretty sure the right choice was going to be *Pride & Prejudice*. She distinctly remembered Darla mentioning watching that with Monica in the past when she had been upset.

Monica emerged from the kitchen with a second glass of wine and a pair of forks, but without the wine bottle. She handed over a glass and a fork, and Marty popped open the lid of the pie box and set it down on the coffee table. Plates were overrated anyway. That was what the box was there for.

Just as predicted, Monica fished *Pride & Prejudice* out of one of the stacks of movies and popped it into the Blu-ray player, although she barely paid any attention to it as it started, instead staring down at her wine glass and she slowly tipped the contents of it from one side to the other. Distractedly, she sat down on the rug in front of the coffee table, and Marty followed suit.

"Is it bad that it sort of felt like a letdown?" Monica finally asked. "I know I was planning on breaking it off anyway, but just... the way it happened seemed so anticlimactic. Like he had to pull the rug out from under me one last time." She huffed out a quiet laugh and sipped her wine. "Oh, man. That makes me sound terrible."

"No," Marty protested, "I know what you're getting at. But at the same time, it's probably for the best. One less burden you had to worry about, on top of everything else."

"I guess." Monica sighed. "I think what I'm most upset about isn't even the breakup itself, really," she admitted, swirling her glass absentmindedly. "I never should have let it drag on for so long, you know? I've been wishing things were different for months, and instead of doing something about it, I just kept hoping that one of these days, he would change. I should have just changed the situation myself."

"You can't blame yourself for having faith in the people you love," Marty argued. "Besides, it's not like you were the only one in charge of the relationship. Connor was just as capable of communicating or taking steps to change things, and it still took him two years to actually do that."

"I suppose you're right," Monica mused, although she still sounded unconvinced. She busied herself by taking a long sip of her wine.

Marty's phone chose that moment to start ringing. She checked it quickly, and saw an unfamiliar number with a California area code on the screen. She rolled her eyes, immediately assuming it was a spam call, and rejected the call. If it was like the last two dozen, they probably wanted to talk about her car's extended warranty.

Setting her phone down on the coffee table and ignoring it, Marty turned her attention back to Monica.

"Weren't you and Connor planning on starting a B&B together?" she asked, and finally took a sip of her own wine. It was red and sweet enough that it nearly disguised the fact that it was definitely not an expensive bottle.

"With a reading room, yeah," Monica confirmed, nodding her head.

"Well, from where I'm sitting, it looks like there's no reason to hold off on that anymore," Marty pointed out. "If Connor's not in the picture anymore, then you don't need to keep sitting on your hands and waiting for him before you can start doing what you really want to be doing."

Monica was quiet for a moment, clearly thinking hard about what Marty had just said. "I suppose it would be a pretty good distraction," she mused after a moment. "Figuring out everything I would need to do to actually get the ball rolling, and all of that."

"It doesn't have to be just a distraction," Marty pointed out. "You aren't just biding your time until your partner has time to humor you. You can do this on your own. You can do whatever you want to now!"

Monica stared at her, blinking slowly, as if the idea of just doing it herself hadn't even occurred to her until that moment.

"It can be the start of a whole new chapter," Marty carried on, "instead of some intermission. You can do whatever you want! Paint the walls orange! Build an entire room just out of hardcover books!"

Slowly, Monica smiled, and it was the most genuinely happy Marty had seen her looking in days.

"I can just do it myself," she repeated slowly, like she was turning the idea over in her mind, letting it percolate for a moment longer. "I don't need to wait for anyone, or for... permission or whatever. I just need to start doing my research, and let the ball start rolling."

"It will be incredible!" Marty gushed, brandishing her fork toward Monica. "And don't forget—you're not entirely by yourself. You have friends who would love to help make your dreams a reality. I have it on good authority those friends would *insist* on helping, actually."

Laughing quietly, Monica knocked her own fork against Marty's, and finally they turned toward the pie, digging their forks into it still in the box. The crust was golden brown and perfectly flaky, and it was perfectly sweet and tart at the same time. Finally, between the realization, the pie, and the movie still playing in the background, Monica seemed more like herself.

They turned their attention to the movie finally. Over the course of it, they finished off the bottle of wine and ate what was probably an ill-advised amount of pie, and Marty wasn't even going to think about what sort of heartburn she was going to have at three o'clock in the morning. It had been worth it.

As the credits rolled, Monica carried their empty wine glasses, the forks, and what was left of the pie into the kitchen, leaving Marty alone in the living room. Marty picked up her phone from where it had been abandoned on the coffee table and checked her email, mostly for something to fill the sudden quiet.

Her eyebrows shot up as she saw the newest email in her inbox. It was addressed to "Ms. Marty Sims." That alone was strange enough, but even stranger was the fact that it was from Sharp's Design Company. Even on the east coast, Marty had certainly heard about the California-based interior design company.

She had won a front-page feature in a magazine as part of a contest, but that had been months ago.

She had been proud of it, of course, but it hadn't impacted her life much, and she had nearly forgotten all about it. But apparently someone all the way in California had seen her spread, and they wanted to set up a time to speak with her.

Remembering the call with the California area code, she quickly pulled up her recent calls, and saw that the number had left a voice mail. She didn't have time to focus on it just then though. Monica came back into the room, and Marty set her phone back down to think about it later. She still had to be there for Monica for the time being.

Even so, the phone call and the email nagged at Marty's thoughts for the rest of the evening.

* * *

When Wyatt got home that evening, he was the only one there, but that wasn't particularly shocking. Marty had her own life, and he knew Monica was having some issues. It didn't take a rocket scientist to figure out where Marty was.

He filled the various cat bowls, did a few chores in the kitchen, and then flopped down on the couch to relax for a few minutes. He should have known better. Within moments, he was swarmed. Trouble clambered up to sit on top of his head. Bertram climbed over the back of the couch to curl up in the gap between Wyatt's head and shoulder. Macy curled up in a perfect circle on his stomach. And Peaches, who liked most people but had somehow decided she adored Wyatt more than anyone except for Marty, climbed onto his chest, tucked her legs neatly under herself, and turned into a perfectly formed loaf of orange cream bread—if bread could purr so hard it made Wyatt's chest vibrate, that was.

Wyatt was trapped. Succumbing to his fate, he turned on the TV and watched it from the corner of his eye as best as he could without dislodging Trouble or Bertram.

When Marty got home, that was how she found all of them.

"Comfy?" she asked, taking a photo on her phone as she did. Her timing was perfect. Immediately after the camera clicked, the cats began to stretch and abandon their human perch to say hello to her.

"How's Monica?" Wyatt asked instead of answering, rather than explaining the crick that had developed in his neck.

"I think she'll be all right," Marty replied, scooping Peaches up off the floor as she did. Trouble,

Bertram, and Macy all stared up at her from in front of her feet.

"Don't let them trick you," Wyatt warned. "I fed them." He rolled his eyes. "Glad to hear Monica's doing... okay, I guess."

"She just needed a bit of a reminder that she's allowed to live her own life without waiting for someone else to show up and jumpstart it," Marty replied, nuzzling the top of Peaches' head for a moment before setting her back down.

She had scarcely said hello to the other cats yet, and she sounded just a bit distracted, for anyone who knew what to listen for. Wyatt's eyebrows rose slightly.

"Did anything else happen?" he asked, finally sitting up properly on the couch.

Marty smiled bashfully at him. "You could tell that easily?"

"I'm very observant," he replied, carefully not mentioning that one time he'd accidentally brought Trouble to work because he hadn't noticed the cat asleep in his bag.

Marty snorted, but she didn't call him on it. She got her phone out, pulled up a message, and passed it over to him with a cheerful, "Have a look for yourself."

Wyatt read the message, but it didn't really clear up anything. He spotted that the address on the letterhead was in California, but he didn't recognize the name of the company.

"You're going to need to elaborate a bit," he admitted, handing Marty's phone back to her.

Marty laughed gently. "I wasn't sure what it was about at first either," she assured him. "It's an interior design company—a big one! They left me a voice mail, and I listened to it on the way home. They want to talk to me about my designs!"

Quickly, Wyatt got to his feet, sweeping Marty into a hug that lifted her off of her feet. She laughed and squirmed in his grasp as he said, "That's amazing! What do they have in mind?"

"I'm not sure!" Marty replied, her voice breathless with laughter, as Wyatt set her feet back on the floor. "They didn't say in the email or the voice mail. I'll have to call them back to ask a few follow-up questions."

Wyatt hurried into the kitchen, and he emerged again a few moments later with two glasses of champagne.

"This calls for a celebration," he declared, handing Marty one of the glasses.

"We don't even know what it's about yet!" she protested, even as she accepted the glass from him.

"Big companies don't message you out of the blue just to say they don't like you," Wyatt pointed out dryly.

"Fair, fair," Marty conceded with another laugh, and she held her glass out to toast before taking a sip.

Whatever it was, it sounded like it was going to be big news. Big news would almost certainly disrupt the happy, content little world they had been building for themselves. But Wyatt pushed that thought aside. They could deal with it later.

Even if he didn't particularly want anything to change just then, it was always amazing to see Marty so excited about something.

CHAPTER SIX

Thursday mornings were often slow in the library. Most people were still at work, so there weren't many patrons coming and going.

When eleven o'clock rolled around, Monica was sitting down for an early lunch, letting her thoughts roam where they pleased. Surprisingly, most of her thoughts were not still hung up on Connor, and she wasn't even particularly sad at that moment. Time healed all wounds, after all, and this one was no different.

What her thoughts did keep circling, however, was the conversation she and Marty had had a little over a week ago. At the time, it just seemed like a consolation, but the more she thought about it, the more she realized that there was nothing holding her back from finally doing everything she wanted.

Well, not quite "nothing." Money was something to think about, as well as an actual location. Whale Harbor was small, and she couldn't just accept any old property as a B&B. There were still hurdles in front of her, but there was no reason she couldn't start putting more serious thought into it.

Of course, that did mean that she was thinking more about what sort of location she *would* like for a B&B than she had ever thought about it before. It would have to be in good condition. She wasn't against doing some sprucing up a few minor repairs, but she didn't want to buy a fixer-upper that would still be requiring repairs six years on.

It would have to be cozy. Warm and quaint, with bookshelves in every room and decor inspired by her favorite books. Marty would surely have some ideas about that. There would be no electronics other than the lights and the computer at the front desk. If she wanted to encourage people to read more and engage with each other, then it meant she had to get them off of their phones, although she supposed she could make an exception for e-readers, even if she personally thought there was no way to replace the feel and smell of a real book. It couldn't be too small either, if she wanted to comfortably fit more than one or two guests at a time. Cozy chairs were a must too —the kind you could curl up in for hours.

And it would have to have good scenery. It wouldn't do if the guests looked out the windows and all they saw was a house on either side and the street in front. There would have to be something unique about where it was located.

She couldn't help but think that if there was a place in Whale Harbor that met those specifications, she would have heard about it already. After all, it sounded like the sort of thing Lori would have been obsessed with, and Marty and Darla hadn't mentioned anything about their mother having a new pet project.

Despite that, she had been thinking about it for too long to just push it out of her thoughts. Forgetting about her lunch for a moment, she grabbed her phone and started looking at real estate listings in the area. She wasn't expecting any miracles, and just as she expected, there weren't a ton of available listings in or around Whale Harbor. She supposed she could have widened the search parameters, but she wasn't willing to get too far outside of town. Most of what she did see was exactly what she expected to see: small, single-family homes that had likely first belonged to fishermen. They were all in fairly good condition, but they also weren't what she was looking for.

She kept scrolling, just to say that she didn't give up, and that was when she saw it. She found her white whale, in the form of a four-bedroom, two-story Usonian summer home on the outskirts of Whale Harbor, just before the cutoff to Blueberry Bay.

It had been built in the nineteen-fifties, with a backyard made up of seagrasses that blended into sand before opening up onto the beach. There were gardens in the front yard, framing the walkway and the driveway, although they were minimalist and begging for a bit of color. It had a small patio, a kitchen, a family room, an office, and three-and-a-half bathrooms. If she had to guess, it had been built for one of the owners of one of the fishing companies to use when they weren't down south for the winter.

By all rights, it should have been light years out of Monica's budget. But when she saw the price it was listed at, her eyes went wide.

It was certainly more than the small fishing homes

she had scrolled past, but it wasn't unreasonable. Maybe because the backyard was so untamed. Maybe because it would certainly need some modernizing in the kitchen and bathrooms. Maybe because it just generally would require a bit of TLC. None of that was unreasonable though, and it had so much potential. She could already imagine the family room being converted into a communal library, and the office being turned into a private reading room.

Maybe she could ask Braden to help with the repair work. She knew he was good at that sort of handiwork, considering the renovations to Gabrielle's house, and as far as she could tell, it seemed like he was planning on sticking around for at least a little while longer.

Then again, maybe she was getting a bit ahead of herself. She hadn't seen the house in person yet. She hadn't taken any steps to actually GET the house. But she supposed she could change that...

She checked the time to make sure her lunch break wouldn't drag on too long, and she called up Lori Sims. As far as she was aware, Lori had gotten back from her cruise in just the last couple of days. The phone rang for a moment before it was answered.

“This is Lori Sims speaking. May I ask who’s calling?”

“Hi, Mrs. Sims,” Monica replied, suddenly feeling bashful, like she was back in high school, hanging out with Darla after class. “It’s Monica.”

“Oh, Monica! Hello, dear! How can I help you? Is everything all right?”

“Everything is fine,” Monica assured her. “How was your cruise?” she asked, not wanting to charge immediately into discussing work. It seemed like it would be a bit rude.

“It was amazing,” Lori replied, with a slow, pleased sigh. “I think my girls were expecting me to have some sort of love affair on the ocean, and that didn’t quite happen, but I had a fabulous time.”

“All the best people in town are single, anyway,” Monica replied. She felt unsure for a moment, worried that maybe the joke was too soon. She felt better enough to say it, but other people could be so awkward about that kind of thing.

But Lori just laughed and agreed with a pleasant, “Too true. Now, what did you need, dear?”

“I was actually hoping to get a closer look at a house that’s for sale,” Monica replied.

“Oh?” Lori still sounded pleasant, but the levity had quickly bled out of her voice as she entered work mode. Monica could hear some shuffling around on the other end, and the sound of a pen scratching. "What's the address?"

"75 Mulberry Street," Monica recited. "It's barely even in Whale Harbor still."

"I know the one," Lori assured her. "It's a beautiful house. Are you looking to move?"

"Nothing like that," Monica answered. "It's a bit much to say over the phone though, and I don't want to get ahead of myself without even seeing the property myself."

"Then you'll have to tell me all about it when you see the house. Does Tuesday morning work?" Lori asked. "I can fit you in around ten."

"That's perfect," Monica assured her. She hadn't actually checked her schedule for next week yet, but she would make it work regardless. Now that she was actually thinking about the B&B, she wanted to get a move on it as quickly as she could, before she could chicken out.

She heard a few more pages shuffling and the pen on paper again, before Lori confirmed, "All right, then. I'll see you on Tuesday at ten. I'll make sure you get the best look at the house as you can, and you can tell me all about what you're planning."

"Sounds great." Monica sighed, relieved. Now

that it was scheduled, it felt more real suddenly. "I'll see you then."

Once they hung up, Monica turned her attention back to the real estate listing, scrolling through the photos one more time. It really was such a lovely house, even if it needed a bit of love.

She supposed Marty was right. This wasn't just going to be some idle distraction. It would be the start of a whole new chapter.

At six o'clock on Thursday evening, Braden opened the door to his mother's house and stepped inside. He could smell dinner cooking, right on schedule, like every day before it. Knowing that Gabrielle was in the kitchen and that she didn't like leaving the stove unattended—as much as she said she loved the gas stove, she had been a bit squirrelly about it for as long as Braden could remember—he kicked his shoes off by the door and headed straight into the kitchen.

Thomas was already in the kitchen when Braden stepped into the room, setting the table.

"You're just in time!" Gabrielle exclaimed. She had known Braden was going to be there, but every time she saw him, it was like she hadn't seen him in weeks.

"A man has to keep his word," Braden replied as he began to help moving side dishes to the table, his voice solemn and earnest enough to make it obvious it was a joke.

Thomas rolled his eyes in mild, good-natured exasperation.

"I'm sure it was such a chore, to pull you away from your work for dinner," he returned wryly.

Braden brought an overly-earnest hand to his chest. "I was willing to make that sacrifice."

"And how was work today, anyway?" Thomas asked, leaning on the counter now that the table was set and it seemed Gabrielle was nearly done cooking.

"Well enough," Braden replied, shrugging one shoulder. "Nothing too exciting happened, unless you count us bringing one of those little brown birds back to shore, but I like working for the fishing company more than I expected. Even with the early start."

"What about that house you've been working on?" Thomas asked. "For the... Clearwaters?" he clarified, even if he evidently wasn't entirely sure of their last name himself. The family hadn't been in Whale Harbor for long, after all.

"I've only just gotten started, but so far, it seems like everything is going well." Even if he liked working on the fishing boat, architecture had still been his bread and butter for a long time. He had been happy to have another project to jump into so soon after finishing the renovations on his mother's house. "It doesn't look like I'm going to run into anything unexpected, so it should mostly just be a bit of modernizing."

"Well, your work on my house was amazing," Gabrielle chimed in, turning off the gas and finally turning away from the stove. She reached for a dish to scoop the veggies she had been sautéing into. "If you need any good references, you know I'll always be happy to put in a good word for you."

"She already talks you up to all of her friends," Thomas added wryly.

Chuckling, Braden said, "Good to know I can always count on your recommendation."

"Will you be picking up any other contractor jobs after this one?" Thomas asked. "It would be a pity not to, if you enjoy the work. Too many people get stuck doing jobs they can't stand for any of us to start passing up jobs we love."

"I hadn't really put much thought into it," Braden admitted. "I'm taking it a contract at a time."

"Well, if you do," Gabrielle added, as she pulled the casserole out of the oven, "keep an eye open for any pretty young ladies too. It's been half an eternity since you dated anyone. I'm starting to worry." She carried the casserole over to the table and set it down on a trivet. At last, the three of them finally took their seats.

"You're only saying that because you're in love," Braden accused playfully. "You think everyone else should be too."

"I want what's best for everyone," Gabrielle said simply, making it clear she thought her logic was untouchable. "Casserole, dear?" she asked, already getting a healthy scoop of it.

Letting the topic drop, Braden held his plate out for his mother to pile with food.

Unbidden, his thoughts drifted back to Monica. He hadn't seen her since that awkward meeting at the library. He could still remember how sad she had looked, and he had overheard just enough of her phone conversation to know what it had been about. It was a pity. She was a sweet woman, and she deserved to feel like she was being treated well. Even so, he also couldn't help but to think that her ex-boyfriend hadn't appreciated her as much as he should have, so it was probably for the best that they had gone their separate ways.

But that was a thought exercise for another time. He didn't need to be thinking about how... someone should treat Monica Grey in a relationship. He pushed those thoughts away, focusing instead on the conversation going on around the table. That wasn't the sort of thing to dwell on at a family dinner.

CHAPTER SEVEN

Saturday was always a busy day at the Marine Center. Most parents didn't have work. The kids weren't in school. Most people didn't have to worry about church. Consequently, the Marine Center was packed with families every weekend.

That wasn't a bad thing, of course. Rick loved knowing how popular the Marine Center was, and he loved knowing it was doing its job to educate people. It was amazing that it was as well-utilized as it was. However, it did mean that there was always a lot of cleaning to be done on Saturday.

Rick was scrubbing small, grubby handprints off the glass of the catfish tank when Jordan strolled by. He had an expectant look on his face, like he was waiting for something. It was obvious enough that

Rick could tell just from Jordan's reflection in the glass.

"How did your date go last night?" Rick asked, since it seemed like the most obvious thing he would want to talk about.

True to form, Jordan pretended to swoon, swaying backward for a second before straightening back up. "It was incredible," he replied, as if his initial reaction left any doubts about it. "We wound up just hanging out and talking for so long that the waiters all started giving us the stink eye over it."

"And you've even gone out with this one more than twice," Rick observed. "Has this one finally earned the title of girlfriend?"

Jordan waved it off dismissively. "Man, that is so far ahead of where we are right now," he scoffed. "We haven't even decided to be exclusive yet. We get along, and that's great, but I don't know if she's, like, my soul mate." He shrugged. "Neither of us are going anywhere quickly. If it happens, it happens, but we're not going to rush into titling something just so we can say 'look, we're grown-ups!' We're already adults, and adults can take all the time they want."

"Fair enough," Rick agreed, before he chuckled wryly. "Meanwhile, I'm trying as hard as I can to become an old married man, but we can't even set a date for it."

Jordan snorted. "You are so head over heels. You're going to get cooties all over the fish. We don't have the equipment to clean that up."

"A harsh accusation, but one I can't even argue with." Rick chuckled. "I am, as the kids say, head over heels."

Jordan arched an eyebrow and leaned one shoulder against the wall beside the catfish tank. "So what's the hold up, then?"

"Nothing terrible," Rick replied. "Both of us want to get married, but weddings take a lot of time to plan, and time is something that neither of us have had in abundance lately."

"Oh, yeah. You have to finish your shift, drink your warm milk, and be in bed by eight p.m.," Jordan replied slyly.

Rick swatted at him with the cloth he was using to scrub the glass, only for Jordan to hop back a step, out of range. Rick shook his head, running a hand through his dark blond hair.

Sly smile still in place, Jordan took a step closer again and leaned in conspiratorially. "Would getting home early for a change give you a chance to talk this stuff out?" he asked. "By my reckoning," he looked at his wrist as if he were wearing a watch, "if you leave now, that should be plenty of time to at least get the conversation going, and I can finish up for you here." He gestured loosely at the cleaning supplies.

"I'm not asking you to do my job for me, just because I'm short on time lately," Rick protested.

"Yeah, that's why I'm *offering*," Jordan replied, refusing to be swayed.

Rick hesitated for a moment, before asking, "You're sure you don't mind?"

Jordan shrugged. "You've covered for me tons of times. What goes around comes around, or whatever."

Rick sighed, some tension he hadn't even been aware of easing out of his shoulders, and dropped his cleaning rag into the bucket by his feet.

"I owe you one," he insisted, stepping away from the catfish tank.

"Yeah, yeah." Jordan waved him on his way. Rick was pretty sure Jordan was never actually going to call in any sort of favor, but he was sure an opportunity to even the score again would pop up at some point in the future.

With a final, "Thanks!" Rick turned and left the Marine Center at a jog.

The trip home was uneventful, and when Rick

got home, Darla was already there. She greeted him with a startled, "Oh! You're back early!" and a kiss, as if it was so strange for them to both be home and awake at the same time.

It sort of was though, as much as Rick didn't like thinking about it. That was the entire problem.

"How's everything at the Marine Center?" Darla asked, pulling Rick over to the couch by his arm. While she sat down carefully, Rick flopped down much less gracefully.

"Everything is fine. You know how Saturdays can be, but it's nothing out of the ordinary. How's set-up at the museum going?" he asked.

Darla groaned and sank back on the couch. "There is so much that needs to be overseen and so much paperwork that needs to be done, and it seems like none of it can ever be done at the same time." She sighed and straightened up again. "But it's going as well as can be expected. The first steps are always the hardest."

Rick hummed in agreement, and the two of them lapsed into comfortable silence. After a moment, Rick started to ask, "Do you suppose we could—?" just as Darla said, "It seems like we've finally got time—"

Both of them stopped talking simultaneously and

stared at each other for a second, before breaking into laughter.

"You first," Darla insisted.

"We're both home at the same time," Rick pointed out. "We could put some thought into picking a date for the wedding."

"That's what I was going to say!" Darla exclaimed, sitting up straight on the edge of the couch. She had that look on her face that she always got when she was preparing to give something her all, her chocolate brown eyes shining brightly.

So of course, that was when her phone started beeping and buzzing as she got a slew of text messages all at once. She grabbed the phone and checked it, her shoulders slumping slightly as she said, "Or, I guess we'll have to take another raincheck." She turned the phone around to let him see the messages. "A delivery scheduled for tomorrow turned up today, and I need to go deal with it. I'm sorry."

"These things happen," Rick replied. They had both learned that lately. "We'll have time later."

Reluctantly, Darla stood up from the couch, leaning over to kiss Rick again before straightening up to her full height.

"See you later." She sighed, before she headed for the door again.

Rick waited until he heard the front door open and then close again before slumping back into the couch with a groan.

Monica had been interested in many things in her life. She loved books. She loved learning new things. She loved surfing. She loved hiking. Few things in life were better than laying out in the sun on the sand with a good book. But one thing she had not taken too much interest in previously was business and the finer details of it.

She knew she should have started looking into it earlier. She and Connor had been planning to start a business together, theoretically, regardless of anything else that had happened. It had just never seemed like the right time to start learning. If she pushed too hard about the B&B, she had been convinced that Connor would pull away even faster.

Now though, she was up to her elbows in business books. She swore, she had raided half the business section of the library, and she had spent all of her free time pouring over the books and absorbing as much information as she could, even at work. While the idea was to run the B&B full time in the future, she still worked at the library, and if nothing else, that made gathering her reading materials convenient.

There were permits and business licenses, and the list went on and on, and she was only just beginning to wrap her head around what paperwork she would need. Maybe a talk with Marty would help. Her friend had opened her own shop, after all...

With a groan, she pushed the current book away from her, across her kitchen table. She had been at it all day, and she had earned a break. It was a Saturday. It was warm out. It was a perfect afternoon for some ice cream.

She got up from her chair, stepped into a pair of sneakers at her door, and grabbed a light jacket just in case, before making the short walk to her favorite ice cream shop. She had been there enough that she was used to the sometimes eccentric flavor names, and she didn't think anything of it when she ordered fish flakes. It was coconut ice cream, filled with flakes and shavings of dark chocolate and macadamia nuts.

She lifted the little plastic spoon from the cardboard cup for her first bite as she left the shop, only to pause when she saw Braden. Her face warmed, and she wasn't sure if it was because she knew she thought he was attractive or because of the state he saw her in at the library. Both options seemed likely. She shoved her spoon into her mouth and tried to focus on that, instead.

She didn't have time to get too worked up before Braden spotted her, and he grinned as if he had been looking forward to seeing her again. Monica shooed that thought away. There was no sense in getting ahead of herself.

"Fancy seeing you here," Braden remarked as he made his way over to her. "What do you have there?"

"Fish flakes," Monica replied, as if it was a completely normal thing to say.

Braden stared at her for a moment, before his eyes darted down to the little cup of ice cream, his eyebrows drawing downward in gradually growing skepticism.

"Have you never eaten ice cream here?" Monica asked, slightly incredulous. "They have all kinds of strange names for the flavors. You have to try it."

"Okay," Braden agreed cautiously, followed by, "Lead the way, then."

Monica blinked at him. She hadn't really meant to escort him, and even if she had, she certainly hadn't meant *right at that moment*. But now that she was thinking about it, it seemed like a good idea.

"All right," she agreed, and she wrapped one hand around his elbow. "You're in for a treat, then." She pulled him back toward the ice cream shop and through the door.

There were a few people scattered around, inside and out, enjoying their own ice cream, and a short line had built up at the counter. Monica decided to use it to her advantage and pulled Braden over to the ice cream case, where she finally let go of his arm to jab a finger at the case.

"Pick your poison."

Braden stared at the rows of different flavors of ice cream like a scholar being handed a Mad Libs book for the first time.

"Frozen Fanta-Sea," he read, with all the caution of a first-time bomb technician. Monica wasn't sure if his wariness was over the name or the fact that it was alarmingly neon orange.

"Try this one!" Monica suggested, pointing a finger at the case.

"The..." Braden paused to read the label. "... Spicy Ginger Pineapple Extravaganza?"

She nodded cheerfully and motioned for a worker to come over.

Within a few moments, Braden was holding a tiny sample spoon of the pale yellow, slightly lumpy ice cream. Slowly and cautiously, he put it in his mouth. He didn't have a reaction at first, but then a split second later, he clapped a hand over his mouth to avoid spitting it out. Monica covered her mouth with one hand to keep from laughing at him.

Spicy Ginger Pineapple Extravaganza, as the name implied, had a great deal of elements to it, but its base was ginger and it had plenty of ginger bits in it. It was the spiciest flavor on the list. Braden fanned his mouth with one hand, stunned by the strange contrast between the cool ice cream and the spicy flavor.

The teenage employee behind the counter smirked slightly as he asked, "So, do you just want a scoop of vanilla?"

While Braden cleared his throat, trying to figure out if he should be insulted by the question or not, Monica took pity on him.

"He'll have a scoop of the Darkest Night," she told the employee. Then she glanced at Braden and added, "Don't worry. It's really good."

When the cup and the scoop of dark brown, speckled ice cream was handed over, Braden eyed it warily for a moment, before cautiously taking a bite and finally relaxing. It was dark chocolate with three different kinds of chocolate chunks in it. "This is delicious," he admitted. Monica smiled happily.

Another influx of customers was arriving, so they took their ice cream back outside. They picked a direction on the sidewalk and started walking.

"So, feeling any better after the last time I saw you?" Braden asked when they had moseyed a short way down the street.

Monica chuckled. "Surprisingly, yes. I've found something better to focus my attention on, although it's a bit too soon for me to start talking about it." It seemed a little presumptuous to start telling everyone and their uncle 'I'm going to start a B&B' when she hadn't even seen the house in-person yet.

"Ah." Braden hummed knowingly. "It's always nice early on, when you're the only one who knows what a project is. When it's just yours."

Monica nodded in agreement. "Did you have projects like that before? You were in D.C., right?"

"Occasionally, but for the most part, the entire team had to know about everything." He rubbed the back of his head with his free hand, suddenly seeming sheepish. "I'm sure that contributed to some of the tension."

Monica's eyebrows rose. "Didn't get on with your coworkers?"

"Sometimes I was certain I had a better way of getting something done, but it wasn't the standard way of doing it. And sometimes I had things to say about that."

"Perfectly polite things," Monica guessed wryly.

"Very colorfully polite," Braden agreed. As if to change the subject, he asked, "Hey, do you want lunch? I haven't really eaten today, other than this." He gestured with his half-eaten cup of ice cream.

They had meandered down the sidewalk far enough that they were standing in front of a bistro. Monica had known of it, but not actually eaten there before. She usually opted for the *Clownfish Eatery* or *Seastar Espresso* as her go-tos, but she was always down to try something new.

They hurriedly finished their ice cream, waited for the brain freeze to dissipate, and headed inside, where a polite young woman seated them and brought them their menus.

They chatted aimlessly at first, until the waitress came to take their orders. As she whisked their menus away, Braden finally asked, "So, what was that whole situation at the library about?"

Monica sighed and admitted, "Just the inevitable

happening, I suppose. Honestly, it probably would have happened a lot sooner if we had been in the same city." It almost felt good to admit it. "Being so far away meant I was always glad just to talk to him, so I wasn't really focusing on all the things that made us ill-fitting for each other."

"Well, now the world is your oyster," Braden said. "What will you do with it, other than your mystery project?"

Monica huffed out a quiet laugh. "Probably the same as usual. Right now, I'm mostly waiting for it to be warm enough to surf."

Braden perked up slightly though he paused as their food was delivered to the table.

"You surf?" he asked, as the waitress left once again.

"Oh, yeah," Monica confirmed. "All summer, usually. I've been surfing since I was little, even if I wasn't actually any good at it until high school." She picked up half of her sandwich. "Do you?" she asked, before taking a bite.

"When I can," he replied. "Which I guess will be more often now. It's been too cold since I got here for me to pick it up again, and there isn't exactly any good surfing in D.C., so it's been a while. Catch any particularly great waves?"

"Yes, but you can't tell anyone," she replied, leaning in conspiratorially.

Mimicking her, Braden leaned in too. "My lips are sealed."

"Around the back of the lighthouse, there's a little beach. The rocks make kind of a C-shape around it, so it's hard to spot most of the time, so no one checks on it much," Monica explained. "I caught some of the most amazing waves of my life back there, and I was the only one there."

"Probably because I'm pretty sure it's illegal to be back there," Braden observed wryly. "Your secret is safe with me."

"What about you?" Monica asked. "Where was your best surfing?"

"A couple friends and I went to Hawaii for spring break in college," he replied, after a moment of thought. "We didn't go to any of the beaches known for professional surfers or anything, or we probably would have broken our necks, but the public beaches there still had some of the best surfing of my life."

"Hawaii!" Monica exclaimed. "That's much fancier than my lighthouse spot."

"Ah, but yours is more convenient," Braden pointed out. "That's valuable insider knowledge."

"True, true."

The waitress chose that moment to cruise by and check on them, and as she left, the conversation started to meander. It was a bit surprising, really. It had been ages since Monica had found it so easy to talk to someone other than her core group of friends. Even before she realized there was anything wrong with her and Connor, their conversations had been getting pretty stilted.

It seemed as if no time passed at all before they finished their food, paid, and continued walking along the street, aimlessly chatting as they went.

As much as she knew she shouldn't, Monica couldn't help but compare Braden to Connor even more as they kept talking. When they were actually together, Connor and Monica had been able to talk about anything for hours the way she was now, with Braden. But they hadn't been together all that often, and the rest of the time, Connor had been very *to the point*. If the conversation didn't seem like it was actively building toward a point, he tended to brush it off or hurry through it.

Braden, by contrast, seemed perfectly happy to tell Monica about the time in high school when he'd pranked the school with a few thousand crickets.

"That was *you*?" Monica squawked at him as he

laughed. She remembered that; it had been the talk of the town for months.

"Yup," he confirmed. "Sure was."

As the conversation continued, Braden seemed just as happy to listen to Monica's stories, grinning as she described the time she'd had to hide in a soggy pit for fifteen minutes so the lighthouse keeper wouldn't catch her on her secret beach.

It seemed as if hardly any time had passed at all, and yet suddenly they had moseyed all the way to Main Street, and it was very nearly dinner. Monica only checked the time when she realized that the sky was beginning to turn from blue to pink and dusty purple, and her eyes went wide as she saw how late it had gotten.

"Oh, shoot," she huffed, shoving her phone back into her pocket. "I need to get going. It was great getting to talk to you though!"

The break had been nice, but she still had a lot of research to get through. The idea of the B&B was exciting, and she wanted to do it right.

"We'll have to do it again," Braden agreed, smiling crookedly at her. Monica couldn't quite ignore the little flip her heart did at the expression. She had never noticed how charming that lopsided smile was, but now that she saw it, she wasn't sure she'd be able to un-see it... even if she wanted to.

"Definitely! Soon too," she declared, before she turned and started walking.

She only made it a few yards down the sidewalk before she peered back over her shoulder, and found that Braden was watching her leave. Her face warmed, and she bit back a smile before turning away and hurrying off.

CHAPTER EIGHT

Marty couldn't remember a time when she hadn't known Rose. Marty had been working at the *Clownfish Eatery* for ages, and she had even been in Rose's house on a handful of occasions, for work-related reasons and neighborly reasons alike. As far as she could tell, Rose and her husband had kept their house the exact same since at least the seventies. Not that it was a bad thing. Marty thought it was charming.

Still, it meant she had certainly been surprised on Monday afternoon when Rose had wandered into *Sand 'n' Things*, looking pleasantly confused.

It had only taken a few moments to suss out that the older woman wanted to redo the guest room in her home, but that she was a bit at a loss as to how to do that. Her granddaughter would be visiting more often, so Rose wanted to turn the guest room into *her* room. She wanted it to be pretty, but she also wanted it to be something her granddaughter would love and she knew her granddaughter had very different aesthetic sensibilities than her.

"I just don't know what young people like lately," Rose admitted fretfully, entirely free of any sort of irony. "I thought you would be the perfect one to ask for some suggestions!"

Marty quizzed Rose about her granddaughter's interests for a bit, just to establish a baseline. She had met Rose's granddaughter a few times at the restaurant, but she didn't know the girl well. Luckily, Rose was happy to gush about her at length, while Marty occasionally made a note in the little notebook she kept by the cash register.

Marty made a few suggestions that both she and Rose were happy with—a teal, green, and purple rug with a swirling mix of feathers and dragonflies; a blue, green, and sandy beige bedspread; a beige and blue padded desk chair; and an acrylic lamp that looked almost exactly like teal, green, and blue carnival glass but wouldn't shatter if someone bumped into the corner of the desk—and made a few observations to help Rose pick out anything else that jumped out to her, before letting Rose loose on the rest of the shop.

Marty waited by the desk as Rose browsed, until her phone rang. She checked the caller ID and saw a California area code.

"I'll just be in the office if you have any questions," she called to Rose as she headed toward the door to the back office. "I need to take this."

"I'm sure I'll be fine," Rose assured her as she inspected a series of macrame wall hangings.

Once she was in her office, Marty answered her phone, with a pleasant, polite, "Marty Sims speaking."

"Good afternoon, Ms. Sims!" a perky, peppy, most likely over-caffeinated woman replied. "My name is Melody Buckley. I work with *Sharp's Design Company*. I was hoping you had a moment to discuss our previous offer."

"Of course," Marty agreed quickly. "I did want to get some clarification on what was going on. The email and the voice mail I got just said you wanted to discuss my magazine spread."

Melody clicked her tongue, tutting in mild disapproval.

"Everyone is always so needlessly vague, honestly." She sighed. "Then I suppose I won't keep you in suspense." She straightened her shoulders, her cheer returning almost immediately. "What we're interested in is offering you a position with *Sharp's Design Company*. From what we've seen of your work, we believe you would fit in with our company wonderfully, and we believe you would have quite a bit to offer."

Marty's heart hammered in her chest, and she was quiet for a few seconds as she let that information sink in.

"A job?" she asked after a moment, her voice small and quiet. For her entire professional life, she had just been an independent, small-town interior designer, and suddenly one of the largest interior design companies in the country was courting her. Marty felt like the floor was about to fall out from under her and she was going to suddenly wake up back in her bedroom.

"Indeed!" Melody confirmed, her cheer seeming all the louder in the face of Marty's shock.

"Do I have to decide right now?" Marty asked cautiously.

"Oh, of course not!" Melody assured her, with a pleasant chuckle. "It's a big change, we're aware of that. Even just keeping the geography alone in mind and disregarding everything else, it would be quite the adjustment. We're not unreasonable, and we don't want you to feel like we're trying to put you on the spot. You have until the end of next week to decide if you want to move forward, and then we can fly you out to our headquarters so you can get a feel for it, get through the proper interview process, and make a final choice."

Melody's voice dropped to a stage whisper as she added, "Between you and me, the interview would just be a formality. You're a shoo-in if you decide you want to go forward with it."

If nothing else, that made the entire situation sound much more reasonable, and relief rushed over Marty at the assurance that she didn't need to make the decision right then and there. She hadn't even had any time to think about it before.

"That's—amazing," she settled on, and it still felt as if she was waiting to wake up at any moment. "Who should I call when I make my decision?"

Melody began to rattle off her phone number, and Marty snatched up a pen and a scrap of paper from her desk. Once she confirmed that Marty had written the number down, Melody offered a cheery, "I look forward to hearing from you soon, then! Have a good afternoon!" and hung up.

Marty was left standing in her office, holding the

paper in one hand and staring at her phone in the other as she tried to make the entire conversation that had just happened make sense.

She had just been offered a job by *Sharp's Design Company*. It was an incredible opportunity, and she couldn't deny that. At the same time, she also knew that accepting that opportunity would mean moving.

Could she do that? Did she even want to? Whale Harbor had been her entire life, and she couldn't even imagine just picking up and leaving some day. And what about Wyatt? Marty chewed her lip absently as the thoughts whirled around her head.

Suddenly, she was even more grateful that she had time to actually make her decision than she had been a moment ago. She had a lot to think about.

Tuesday was a bright, sunny day. While that was nothing particularly out of the ordinary for the time of year, Monica took it as a good omen all the same, as she got ready to go meet Lori at her prospective B&B. She was finally going to see the house in person, and it was the most excited she had been in weeks.

She was just stepping out her front door when her phone rang. She paused on her front step to answer it, not even checking to see who it was first.

"Monica Grey speaking."

"Hi, Monica," the woman on the other end replied, sounding slightly awkward right out of the gate. "I'm not sure if you remember me, but this is Naomi Warwick, from San Francisco. We met while you were visiting Connor last year."

Monica was quiet for a moment, mind churning to drum up the memory of the woman on the other end of the phone line. "Naomi! Right, right," she acknowledged as the memory slotted in place. She was one of Connor's colleagues, although she worked in a different department. "Hi. What can I do for you?" she asked, bemused.

Naomi had been nice enough while Monica was in San Francisco at the time, but they had hardly interacted at all since then, and other than liking a few posts on social media, they hadn't actually *spoken* to each other at all.

"You were asking me about business licensing while you were here, since you and Connor had been planning to start a business together," Naomi explained. "Thanks to a few new projects at work, I've learned quite a bit about the topic since then, and I thought I would get in touch to see if you were still interested or if it was still relevant to you. I would have given just given the info to Connor to pass along, but I thought that would be a bit awkward, considering you two aren't a thing anymore. Took a bit to remember I still had your number."

"Well, thanks for reaching out. You actually don't know how perfect your timing is." Then she thought of something. Monica's eyebrows furrowed together in confusion. "But, wait—how long have you been thinking about getting in touch with me?" she asked, bewildered. "Connor and I only just recently broke up."

The other end of the phone line was silent for a moment, and Monica felt a worm of dread beginning to wiggle to life in her stomach.

"Oh." Naomi's voice was just a low mumble, as if she wasn't really saying it to Monica, but just happened to be having a private realization while holding the phone. There was a long, awkward pause.

"Are you sure?" Naomi asked quietly, as if it was the only thing she could think to say. She had to have realized it was a ridiculous question, as she didn't actually wait for a response before she kept talking.

"I assumed the two of you had broken up months ago, and he just didn't talk about it," she admitted, and Monica braced herself for whatever she was about to hear next. "I think we all did. He hasn't really said much about you, and one of the girls from marketing has been all over him for the last few months."

Despite bracing for whatever she might hear, Monica's breath still rushed out of her all at once, as if someone had decided to kick her in the chest. She couldn't think of anything to say. Naomi didn't say anything either. Both of them were silent for several moments that felt like they stretched on for hours.

Finally, Naomi broke the silence.

"Look, I... I'll just text you the licensing info, all right? I'll give you some space to... process, or whatever."

"That's fine," Monica mumbled into the phone, her voice working on autopilot.

"I'm really sorry," Naomi offered, sounding about as uncomfortable as Monica had ever heard anyone sound.

"Thank you for telling me," Monica murmured, barely audible, and then she hung up the phone. Her arm fell down to her side, and she stared down at the cement of her front step, gray and gritty between her shoes.

Why hadn't he just broken up with her? It's not as if he would have done it in person. Even when he finally got around to it, he still didn't do it in person. If she had meant so little to him, then why hadn't he just told her, broken it off, and let her start moving on with her life? They had loved each other at some point, or at least she was pretty sure he had loved her before. What had she done to make him so callous? What had she done to deserve him cheating on her for *months*?

The cement between her shoes blurred, and she reached up with her free hand to scrub at her eyes. She took a deep, shuddering breath, and sighed it out slowly, and she repeated the process until her breathing was steady and even, and she knew she would be able to speak without her voice wobbling like a seesaw.

She lifted her phone back up and punched in Lori's number.

"Hi, Mrs. Sims," she greeted when the other woman picked up. She forced some cheer into her voice so Lori wouldn't ask any questions. "Could we reschedule the viewing for another day? I'm having some car trouble. Can I just call you when I know a good time to reschedule?"

"Of course," Lori said kindly. "It's not a problem at all. Just let me know when you're ready to reschedule."

"Okay, great." Monica cleared her throat. "I'll call you soon."

She hung up the phone, shoved it into her pocket, and let the tears fall. Right there on her front step, she scrunched down into a ball, hiding her face against her knees. She was glad none of her neighbors were outside to see her just then. She didn't think any of them would judge her, but they would probably try to come make sure she was okay, and she just didn't have it in her to reassure any of them just then.

After a few minutes, she slowly straightened back up and headed back into her house, letting the door swing closed behind her with a bang.

CHAPTER NINE

Wednesday was a quiet day. The middle of the week usually was. Most people looking to try out a new quad wanted to set some time aside for it, so Fridays and weekends were Wyatt's busiest days.

Despite the relative ease of the day, by that evening, he couldn't push away a sense of unease. He knew Marty well. He certainly knew her well enough to know when there was something on her mind that she wasn't talking about.

She didn't seem sad. She didn't seem angry. She didn't seem upset, per se. But she had hardly spoken since Wyatt had gotten home, and even then, she hadn't said more than a handful of words. They had eaten dinner and watched a movie, and throughout the entire evening, it seemed as if her thoughts were several hundred miles away.

The credits of the movie were rolling and Wyatt was carrying a plate of chocolate chip cookies and two glasses of milk into the room when he finally decided to broach the subject. Marty was staring at the credits as if the list of lighting engineers held all the answers in the universe, until Wyatt nestled one glass into her hands and she snapped back to the present.

"So, are you going to tell me what's on your mind, or should I start playing Twenty Questions?" Wyatt asked, taking a seat on the couch with his own glass. He set the plate down on the coffee table. "Is something wrong?"

Marty picked up a cookie and dunked half of it into her glass. "Not... wrong, no," she answered carefully. It wasn't a particularly comforting answer.

"That clears a lot up," Wyatt said dryly, and Marty huffed a little laugh before she took a bite of her cookie.

Finally, she took a deep breath and said, all in one quick rush, "I finally got to talk to someone from *Sharp's Design Company* and they want to offer me a staff job in San Francisco."

Wyatt stared at her for a few seconds, letting her

words fall into place until they made sense. A staff job meant she would have to work there, wouldn't it? It would require she pick up and move the entire way across the country, if she decided she wanted to take the job.

He knew it was an amazing offer and opportunity for her, but he also couldn't help but to wonder what it would mean for the two of them if she decided she wanted to ultimately leave Whale Harbor and take the job. He didn't want to lose her, but he also didn't want to be the one standing in the way of her dreams. He knew how much her job meant to her.

"I have until the end of next week to decide if I want to go to San Francisco for an interview," Marty continued, "and if I decide to do the interview, I can still decide that the city isn't a fit for me. So, nothing is set in stone yet."

Finally gathering up his wits again, Wyatt asked, "What do you want to do though? Do you want to go for the interview?"

Marty used the rest of her cookie as an excuse to stay silent, mulling over the question as she nibbled around the edge of it before finishing it off in a few quick bites.

"I'm not sure," she admitted once the cookie was

gone. "I know it's an amazing opportunity. Most people in my situation couldn't even dream of having this sort of opportunity just handed to them. I feel like it just wouldn't be smart to pass it by without at least seeing what they have to offer over there." She fiddled with her glass, turning it back and forth between her hands. She looked like she had more to say, so Wyatt waited quietly.

"But what if I got the job?" she asked quietly. Wyatt couldn't tell if she was asking him or asking herself. "I would have to move. Would you move with me?"

Wyatt was quiet at first, his thoughts churning a mile a minute. At first, all he could think about was his father, and how grateful he was that Wyatt was so passionate about the family business. While it was true that the business had grown, they were still a small, family-owned and -run business. Wyatt knew he wouldn't be able to run the current locations from the West Coast. Even thinking about the logistics of it was giving him a headache.

"I'm not sure *Wyatt's Quads* would survive that sort of distance," he pointed out.

"I know." Marty sighed, and there was a concerned little furrow between her brows. Wyatt wanted to smooth it out.

He set his glass down on the coffee table and draped one arm along the back of the couch, making space for her. Marty set her own glass down and scooted over, curling up against Wyatt's side. He wrapped his arm around her.

"It's a lot to think about," Wyatt acknowledged. "But like you said, you don't need to make any decisions quite yet. And I don't have to make any decisions until you do," he pointed out. "So, how about we don't start worrying about it until we know more?"

"I suppose," Marty agreed, her voice partially muffled from where she was tucked against his side.

"And whatever you decide to do, I'll support you," Wyatt assured her, his arm tightening around her. He felt her shift to tuck her head under his chin, her dark curls tickling him pleasantly. "Even if it makes things a little bit more complicated. I know how hard you work and how much you love what you do. If anyone deserves to have their efforts recognized, it's you."

"You're going to give me an ego," she grumbled, still muffled.

"You've earned it," he replied wryly.

It was true. She had earned it. And he fully intended to support her, no matter what she decided to do. But that didn't ease the worry at the back of his mind that he might lose her soon.

* * *

The next few days seemed to pass at a crawl and in an instant. By the time Monday rolled around, Monica could barely even process it. It felt like she had been stuck in a blender full of molasses.

She had spent too much of the last few days thinking about Connor. She didn't like how thoroughly he had wormed his way back into her brain, and he hadn't even had to do anything. But no matter how Monica tried to distract herself, the questions kept swirling through her brain. Her racing thoughts had kept her awake at night, which was part of why she felt so sluggish today.

Who was the woman Connor had been cheating on her with? How could he do it so easily, and still talk to her like normal when they called? If he was so unhappy with her, why didn't he just break up with her before, instead of stringing her along? What had changed that made him finally cut the cord and end things with her?

She almost wished she had quizzed Naomi on the phone, but she knew that wouldn't have been fair to Naomi. She didn't ask to be the one to break the news to Monica. From the sounds of it, she hadn't even realized there was news to break.

Monica snapped back to the moment when a book thumped through the return slot, and she looked up to see Lori Sims on the other side of the desk. Monica blinked at her for a moment, reorienting herself to the fact that she was, in fact, still in the library, at work. She cast a glance at the clock and saw that it was eleven. She had been lost in thought for a couple of hours at that point, apparently.

Lori smiled at her, warm and pleasant. She had wavy red hair and blue eyes, and her makeup and outfit were both perfectly put together. "Hello, dear," she offered. "Have your car troubles been taken care of?"

Monica was confused for a moment, before she remembered the excuse she had given on Tuesday as to why she couldn't see the house.

"Oh, right. Yeah, the car is fine," Monica replied.

Lori didn't say anything else about the car, but there was a knowing shine to her eyes that made Monica feel like Lori was staring right through her.

"Oh, that's good!" Lori exclaimed, clasping her hands together in front of her chest. "I remembered how you used to talk about starting a bed and breakfast, so I assume that's why you're interested in the house on Mulberry. And once I was thinking about it from that perspective, I have to say, it would be the perfect house! There's so much space!"

Monica opened her mouth to reply, but Lori kept speaking, like a very cheerfully determined steamroller. This was probably why Lori had the reputation for being a really effective realtor; she was pleasant, yet seemed unstoppable.

"If your car troubles have been handled, then I have plenty of time on Wednesday to show you the house," she offered, looking at Monica expectantly.

Monica very nearly said no, that she didn't have time, but she bit the impulse back. She had the time. She was just sad and wallowing in it, and she knew it. Even admitting that to herself, she still sort of wanted to say no. After all, was she in any sort of headspace to actually appreciate or analyze the house? As upset as she was, she might very well start finding flaws in every corner and every piece of woodwork.

But she was being ridiculous. She had found what could very well be the perfect house to finally achieve her dream. One day, she could leave the library and run her very own B&B full time, if she just reached out for the opportunities that were in front of her. Was she really going to let Connor steal that from her? Was she going to let him win, after everything else that he had already done? Was she really going to keep putting her life on pause because of him when he wasn't even in her life anymore?

He had lied to her. He had hurt her. And he had left her, months before he had actually broken up with her. But the fact that Monica had been hurt shouldn't stop her from living her own life. It *wasn't* going to stop her from living her own life.

She set her hands on the desk, palms flat on the surface, and took a deep breath. Lori was still watching her expectantly, waiting for an answer. Monica had no doubt that she was ready to start arguing if Monica tried to say no, so it was a good thing that Monica was ready to give her the answer she wanted.

"You said Wednesday, right?" she asked.

Lori's smile brightened. "That I did," she confirmed.

"I think that should work, then," Monica replied. "Wednesday sounds like a good day to see the house."

"Wonderful!" Lori pulled her phone out and quickly began typing something into it, presumably to add Monica to her schedule. "Around one o'clock?" she asked, glancing up over the top of her phone until Monica nodded at her. "Great. Then I'll see you on Wednesday."

"Um, okay. Sounds good."

"Great! Have a good day at work!" Lori called over her shoulder as she turned and left.

Monica watched her go, feeling a bit like she had just been hit by a bulldozer, although in a strangely good way. The bulldozer had Monica's best interests at heart.

Where before her thoughts had been stuck circling around Connor and what he had done, suddenly it was as if every thought of him had been washed away. Monica made sure there were no patrons approaching the desk before she pulled up the real estate listing for the house on the computer again. As she scrolled through the photos, her brain came alive with all of the options ahead of her.

It was true that the B&B wasn't *just* a distraction. It was a new chapter. But that didn't mean it couldn't also be a distraction too. And just because Connor hadn't cared about Monica or the promises they had made together, that didn't mean she couldn't care about herself. She could do this on her own, as a promise to herself.

CHAPTER TEN

It was probably a good thing that Wyatt didn't have any customers right at that moment. Cleaning and doing maintenance on the quads didn't take much thought, and he could do it on autopilot, but customer service required a bit more awareness. At that point, Wyatt was barely aware of anything except the polishing cloth in his hand, the quad in front of him, and his thoughts chasing themselves in circles. Tuesdays weren't the busiest days though, and eight o'clock in the morning was certainly not when most people decided they needed to try out a new quad.

He couldn't stop thinking about Marty's job offer. He had said he would support her, and he had meant it. He would cheer her on regardless of what she decided was best. Even so, he couldn't help but to worry about the possibility of her taking the job and moving across the entire country.

Wyatt had already lost someone who was supposed to be the love of his life when he and his ex-wife divorced. He knew he was beyond lucky to have won Marty's heart at all, especially considering the reservations she'd had about his past, but he didn't think he could go through that sort of loss all over again. And yet there he was, contemplating what he would do if that exact thing happened.

He knew he had found a diamond in the rough with Marty, but he also knew he had to be realistic. If she decided to take the job in San Francisco, he wouldn't stop her. He wouldn't keep her from her dream, but he also knew he couldn't leave. At least for the foreseeable future, he had to stay in Whale Harbor to take care of the business.

So intense was his focus on the brewing trouble that he didn't even notice when someone stepped into the shop until he announced himself.

"Hey."

Wyatt jumped, very nearly dropping the cloth, and turned to see who had walked in, spotting Braden standing casually, his hands in his pockets.

He looked amused at the intensity of Wyatt's distraction.

"Circling the moon today?" he asked, one eyebrow rising.

Wyatt waved it off and tossed the polishing cloth onto the nearest shelf to deal with later. "Just a bit distracted," he replied. "What's up?"

Braden shrugged a shoulder. "Not a ton," he replied. "I just figured I would stop in to say hi. It's been a while."

It was a fair enough point.

"Getting too busy for us little people, now that you're the architect around town." Wyatt sighed, so earnestly lamenting that there was no possible way to take him seriously.

Braden frowned at him lightly for a second, before the expression melted into quiet confusion. "How did you even hear about that? Other than my mom's house, I've barely had time to talk about the other projects I've picked up."

"Anyone who knows your mom knows exactly how many renovation projects you've been hired for," Wyatt informed him, his voice laden with amused sympathy. "She's very enthusiastic."

Braden sighed and pinched the bridge of his nose between two fingers. "I thought she was kidding, but apparently not." He chuckled wryly. "Well, you know how my business is doing. How's business at the ATV Farm?"

"It's going well. The customer base is growing, which is fantastic," Wyatt said. "What about the fishing? Still doing that?"

"Still waking up at a ridiculous hour every morning," Braden said with an over-the-top wince. Wyatt pantomimed pulling off an imaginary hat and holding it to his chest in sympathy, and Braden grinned.

While Wyatt was genuinely glad to hear that things were going well for Braden, he couldn't help but remember that Braden still wasn't sure if he was actually staying in Whale Harbor or not. He wondered if that was a relief for him, since he didn't have to worry about anything like Wyatt and Marty's current concerns.

Wyatt didn't regret putting down roots. He loved Marty and any time he got with her, and he loved Whale Harbor. But nevertheless, he hadn't thought he would need to have this internal debate with himself, about how and where he and Marty would be the happiest. She had seemed so settled in Whale Harbor herself. It had never even occurred to him that she might consider leaving, and he had never expected something like that to potentially uproot his entire life.

"Everything good?" Braden asked, and Wyatt supposed he had to be a bit more distracted than usual.

"Nothing is *bad*," he answered carefully, without elaborating. He wasn't sure how much he wanted everyone else to know what was going on. He wasn't even sure how many people Marty had told about the job offer, and it wouldn't help anything if word got out and everyone in town started acting like she was leaving before she even made up her mind. At the same time, he also needed to talk to someone about it because he wasn't getting anywhere with it on his own time.

Braden arched an expectant eyebrow.

"Marty potentially has a job interview in San Francisco," Wyatt confessed. "It's an amazing opportunity for her, so I get why she doesn't want to just turn it down out of hand, but it's left my foundation feeling a bit rocked."

Braden's eyebrows rose in surprise. "San Francisco?" he repeated. "But Marty's basically a staple of this town, far as I can tell."

"I guess it's not so different from you thinking

you could only reach your full potential as an architect in the city," Wyatt mused.

Braden was quiet for a moment before he spoke again.

"It's a touchy situation. I mean, I still haven't even fully decided if I'm staying or not, but I know I wouldn't trade the relationship I've built with my mom or Thomas for anything," he said, shrugging one shoulder casually. "But at the same time, a good job is something you may very well be doing for the rest of your life until you retire, so I get wanting to make the right decision about it."

All it did was confirm Wyatt's thought that there was no right or wrong choice about the situation. It was just going to keep being complicated. Of course, Wyatt hadn't thought that one conversation with an outside party would clear up the entire situation, but he had at least been hoping it would shed a bit of light on things. Oh well.

He pushed that thought away, instead pulling up a cheeky smile. "Nothing but your relationship with your mom tempting you to stay?" he teased. "Nothing at all? No lady friends that might encourage you to stick around for a while longer?"

Now it was Braden's turn to look like he was

choosing his words carefully. He folded his arms over his chest. "What are you getting at?"

Wyatt shrugged casually, palms up. "There's just been some talk around town, is all," he replied.

"It's Whale Harbor. There's always talk around town," Braden pointed out wryly. "Small town gossip is the closest thing to a local sport around here."

"People have seen you with Monica around town," Wyatt replied. "It looked an awful lot like the two of you were out on a date not too long ago."

Braden huffed out an incredulous laugh. "I'm not sure Monica's really ready for dating quite yet, considering everything else that's happened recently," he said. "I'm not going to push the matter. Besides, we're just friends."

"Those don't have to be mutually exclusive," Wyatt argued. "Marty's my best friend." Even if she did leave, Wyatt couldn't imagine a world where he wouldn't want her in his life. She knew him better than anyone else did, and probably better than anyone else ever would.

Braden fell silent for a moment after that, his expression turning thoughtful, and Wyatt didn't push the subject. These things had to happen naturally, after all.

"Well, I hope everything works out for you soon,"

Braden offered eventually, and the look on his face said that he was still turning their conversation over in his head. "I'll let you get back to tending your herd."

"See you later," Wyatt said. "Tell your mom I said hi."

"Will do," Braden assured him as he left.

Wyatt watched his friend go, his thoughts running in circles like Trouble chasing her own tail.

* * *

Tuesday evening was warm and pleasant as Darla drove home. There was barely a cloud in the sky as it turned purple for the sunset. When she got home, the house was still dark and only her car was in the driveway as she climbed out and headed for the door. Rick was still at work.

The house was quiet as she stepped inside and toed off her shoes, her arms too full to reach down and pull her shoes off the traditional way. She crouched down and bumped the light switch with her shoulder before she headed into the kitchen and began arranging her bounty on the table and counter. Once her hands were free, she started properly arranging everything, making sure everything was neat and easily accessible. They were going to have a lot to do tonight, so it was for the best that everything go as smoothly as possible.

She pulled her phone out as she continued rearranging everything on the table and counter, and she made a quick phone call as she worked. Once the call was over—it was brief and simple, hardly taking any thought from her—she set her phone down on the table and kept making sure everything was perfect.

There were so many things to consider. Maybe she had gone a bit overboard, but she supposed that was better than not being enthusiastic enough.

Eventually, the door opened once again as Rick got home, and Darla turned to face him. As he walked into the kitchen and came to a halt in the doorway, she waited for him to react.

"You've been busy," he remarked after a moment, stepping fully into the room.

"I'm taking matters into my own hands," she replied decisively. "You're officially off duty for the night. All your attention is now on this."

She had covered the table and counter in supplies for planning a wedding. There were magazines and brochures, a corkboard with images and ideas she had found inspiration tacked to it, and a booklet of fabric swatches in different colors and materials.

Rick smiled, happiness glinting in his honey brown eyes—but before he could say anything, the doorbell rang, and instantly he looked wary. Darla supposed he was expecting something else to suddenly interrupt them, but she breezed past him to open the door. She accepted the two bags of Chinese takeout from the delivery driver, handed him a tip, and sent him on his way.

"We don't need to worry about cooking. I don't need to worry about anything with the museum. You're done with work for the evening." She set the bags of food on a free section of the counter and began pulling takeout containers out, setting them on top of the stove as she did. "We finally have time, and we're going to take advantage of it." She handed Rick a cardboard takeout container and a fork before picking up her container of noodles and a pair of chopsticks.

Rick made a point to salute her like she was a drill sergeant before he sat down, but there were no actual complaints. He seemed just as relieved as she was that there was finally time to sit down and start actually planning their wedding.

Despite the entire speech, neither of them

actually said much as first. It felt as if they had barely seen each other for more than ten minutes at a time lately. It was nice to just know they were in the same room as each other, enjoying some fried rice and lo mein together.

"I want to aim for sometime in the fall," Darla said eventually, after enjoying her noodles for a few minutes. "That doesn't leave a ton of time to make any drastic plans, but I don't think we'll be *needing* a ton of drastic plans."

"I figured we were aiming for a small wedding anyway," Rick agreed. "We don't need to have the entire town there, even if it will probably be the talk of the town afterward."

"Yes, I think small is good." Darla nodded thoughtfully. "Honestly, I was almost tempted to do the ceremony on your boat, but that might force us to keep our guest list too small. And besides, you never know when someone might get seasick."

Rick's eyes widened in surprise. "The boat? Really?"

"Well, it was where we had our first date," Darla pointed out with a smile. "Even if we weren't actually *officially* dating at the time. It was where everything started. And I'm comfortable enough on the water now that *I* would be comfortable. But thinking back to how sick I was, I wouldn't want to subject any of our guests to that."

It had taken a lot of conditioning and a lot of lost lunches over the side of the boat, but she was proud of the fact that she had toughed it out until she was used to being on the open water. Once, the rock of the boat and the ebb and flow of the ocean had spelled out nothing but a terrible time. Now it was comforting. She wouldn't feel like some sort of sham or poser, marrying a man who spent so much of his time on the water.

Still, she wasn't sure that her mother and sister had the same sea legs she did, not to mention many of the other potential guests.

Rick smiled at her, and it was such a tender and warm expression that Darla felt tears prick at her eyes.

"I love that idea," he said. "I see why it's probably not practical, but it means a lot that you thought of it."

"I'm glad." She grinned. "I like that I can share that part of your life with you now. I'm not a landlubber anymore."

"Nope, you most certainly are not."

Since they'd crossed the boat off as an option, they batted around a few other ideas, eventually settling on a historic estate not far outside of Whale Harbor. The rest of the evening passed pleasantly, as they discussed decorations and colors and the particulars of the guest list. The more they spoke, the more real it all felt, as if their plans were coalescing into a solid, physical entity right in front of them. As if Darla could reach out and touch it at any moment.

She couldn't wait.

CHAPTER ELEVEN

At twelve-thirty on Wednesday afternoon, Monica left to meet Lori at the new house—the prospective new house. Monica didn't want to get ahead of herself. By one o'clock, her car was pulling into the house's driveway, where Lori's car was already waiting.

Lori hurried down from the front step as Monica got out of the car, and she spread out an arm as she asked, "What do you think? First impressions?"

"It's amazing," Monica breathed, already enamored. It was already apparent it would need work—the cement pavers leading from the driveway to the front step were overgrown, the brick making up the house was a bit dingy, and she could see a layer of dust on the inside of the windows—but she couldn't just ignore the fact that it was a beautiful house. With some power washing and some gardening, it would look like the cover of a novel, which was exactly the effect Monica wanted for her reading-themed B&B.

"There's no sense in lingering out here," Lori decided, ushering Monica along. "Let's head inside."

The entryway wasn't enormous, but it had a coat closet and it was big enough to hold a check-in desk, and it led to a hallway that opened into a kitchen and dining room combo, with a decorative wall dividing it from a living room. Already, there were built-in shelves in the wall, just crying out to be filled with books and surrounded by comfortable chairs and a couch. It hardly even mattered that there was no dishwasher and that the kitchen appliances were out of date. Monica easily pictured how things would look, once they were spruced up.

As they explored from room to room, Monica's excitement only grew. The office had plenty of room for a spacious desk she could run the B&B from. The bathrooms were a bit trapped in the seventies, with tiles of bubblegum pink, but that was nothing that couldn't be fixed. Each bedroom was cozy, and the master had a phenomenal view of the beach behind the house.

"Let's head back out and see the backyard," Lori decided, as if sensing where Monica's thoughts were going. Monica followed her back outside without protest.

The backyard was clearly overgrown. In the photos, Monica had thought the patio in the back was fairly small. Once she was actually standing on it though, it was clear that it was twice the size she had assumed it was. Most of it was simply hidden in the weeds. It had plenty of space for some outdoor chairs and a couch, and even a fire pit for the fall and winter. She could set up a few poles and string lights between them, and it would be perfect. Monica could practically see it in her head.

There were a few trees, but not enough to block the view of the ocean. It was close enough that Monica could hear the waves breaking against the sand. The grass overgrowing the yard gradually gave way to sand, and for a moment Monica wanted to take off at a sprint toward the water, but she knew it wasn't a good time for that.

She turned away from the view, staring at the back of the house instead. Some window boxes wouldn't hurt, but most of the work outside would just be unearthing what was already there and had begun to disappear through neglect.

It was clear it would take a fair amount of work to get the house into shape to be a B&B. Monica had no delusions about that. But she also knew it was all things that she could do. None of it was insurmountable. Her optimism grew and grew.

They headed back inside, and Monica took another lap of the kitchen, the bathrooms, and the bedrooms, just to make sure she hadn't missed anything. Eventually, they wound up standing in the entryway again as Lori asked, "What do you think?"

"It's perfect!" Monica exclaimed. "It's even better than I was hoping. I want to make an offer."

"Wonderful!" Lori gestured toward the door with a smile. "Then we can meet at my office to get the details down, and I can get the ball rolling on that."

Monica's thoughts raced as she headed back to her car and followed Lori's sedan back through town, to her office. It was a big purchase—an enormous purchase. But she had savings. Hopefully she had enough. She was optimistic though. The house had been on the market long enough that she thought her odds were pretty good. It would take nearly everything in her savings, but that was what that account was for to begin with: manifesting this dream. Regardless of whether she had help or was doing it on her own, she had spent years setting money aside for the same purpose.

It was a bit bittersweet, of course. She had always assumed she would be reaching for this dream with Connor at her side, once he was back in Whale Harbor. It was strange to think that she would be doing it on her own. But it wasn't bad. She had enough distance now to admit that Connor would never have been particularly enthusiastic about the B&B, no matter what promises he made. It was always going to be just Monica handling everything. Considering that, it would probably be *easier* to do it without Connor skulking around in the background.

She'd spent enough time waiting on Connor, sitting in the wings and waiting for him to decide when she could finally start to chase her dreams. She didn't need his permission or approval though. She didn't need him to be involved at all.

The bittersweet feeling was fading the longer she thought about it, until she nearly wanted to burst out laughing behind the steering wheel. She kept the urge in check, since she didn't want anyone else on the road to think she had lost her marbles. If she had her entire dream ahead of her, then that also meant she had all the time in the world to celebrate too.

* * *

Wednesday afternoon was bleeding into evening by the time Braden realized how long he had been out on the water. Not on the boat—he had finished up with that for the day hours ago—but on his surfboard.

Water rushed around his ankles as he stood with his board tucked under his arm, shading his eyes with his other hand and squinting into the sunset. It wasn't the most dignified pose, but it was a beautiful sunset. The view combined with the sheer joy of surfing were what he had missed the most when he moved out of Whale Harbor. Despite how long he had been back, he still liked to take every chance he got to appreciate it.

It helped that the waves that day were basically perfect.

Even so, surfing in the dark came with some unique risks, and Braden wasn't about to be *that* reckless. He was just about to head toward the showers when he realized he wasn't the only one still on the beach. He could see a small fire burning out of the corner of his eye. It was curiosity that drew him toward it initially, until he realized the little driftwood fire belonged to Monica and he approached with a bit more enthusiasm. She had her board with her, standing upright with one end of it speared into the sand. As Braden got closer, he could see that she was drinking champagne out of the bottle.

That could be a good thing or a bad thing, especially considering everything else that had been happening, but she didn't look particularly upset as he approached. Tentatively, he assumed the champagne was a good sign.

"Having fun?" Braden asked as he got closer, and he fought a smile off of his face when she jumped slightly, clutching the bottle to her chest before she lowered it. "Sorry," he offered half-heartedly though he didn't feel particularly apologetic. Based on the lighthearted scowl she aimed at him, Monica seemed to sense it. "I didn't see you show up," he observed, propping his board up in the sand.

Monica waved it off casually with one hand and took another sip of champagne. "I called it quits for the evening a while ago," she replied. "Heading back home just seemed like a waste of a good evening."

That was something he had always appreciated about her. There was nothing wrong with an old-fashioned bookworm who just wanted to sit on the couch and read, but Braden appreciated that Monica managed to fit so much else into her life without shutting herself away in some dark, cloistered library. He would have appreciated it slightly more if he'd actually had the chance to watch her surf earlier, but he supposed there would be more chances in the future, most likely. At least, he hoped so.

"A good evening for sitting on the beach and drinking alone?" Braden asked.

Monica gestured expectantly to a patch of empty sand beside her fire with the hand not holding the bottle. Dutifully, Braden dropped down to sit cross-legged in the sand, and he accepted the bottle when Monica passed it to him.

"Now I'm not drinking alone," she pointed out as he took a swig from the bottle. "I'm celebrating," she added, almost conspiratorially.

"Did Connor fall into a hole full of wet cement?" Braden asked, trying his absolute hardest to sound innocent and completely missing the mark.

Monica laughed once, sharp and startled, and flicked a lump of soggy sand in Braden's direction.

"No," she answered, her tone playfully scolding. She accepted the bottle when Braden handed it back. "I bought a house. Well, I put in an offer on a house on Mulberry Street."

Braden's eyebrows rose. "Feeling a bit cramped in your house?" he asked, curious.

Monica was quiet for a moment, looking as if she was debating with herself how much to say, before she said, "I don't want to jinx anything by jumping the gun, but it's always been my dream to start a bed and breakfast." She paused to take another drink before continuing. "I originally planned to start with Connor when he moved back into town, but since that's not going to happen, I didn't see a reason to hold off on it any longer."

"Good for you," Braden said earnestly.

"Nothing's set in stone yet," Monica continued quickly. "I only just put the offer in today, and even if it's accepted, the house will need a lot of work to make it what I want it to be. But... well, it turns out Connor was cheating on me, and I could use the distraction."

She said it so casually that it took a moment for Braden to actually process the words, and then his eyes went wide. "He—what? Seriously?"

Monica shrugged. "It's not that surprising, in retrospect," she murmured.

"That doesn't mean it's *right*," Braden argued. "When you have someone incredible, you don't—" He cut his tirade off. If Monica actually wanted to talk about *that* right then, she likely wouldn't have dropped it into the conversation so lightly. Braden shook his head slightly and, with an effort of will, changed the subject. "What sort of work will the house need?"

Monica smiled at him gently, and maybe a bit gratefully. "Mostly landscaping and modernizing, plus I would need to install a check-in desk and a few shelving units in the bedrooms and communal spaces."

"Making a library-B&B combo?" Braden asked.

"More or less," Monica replied with a chuckle. "Somewhere people can just turn off all the tech and relax, without a neon sign two inches from their face at all hours."

"Sounds nice," Braden mused quietly, before offering, "I could help with the renovations. If your offer gets accepted, I mean."

"I might just take you up on that," she replied, offering him a crooked smile, before her attention turned toward the horizon. The sun had well and truly set by then, leaving the sky a dusty purple. "I should probably get going."

"Yeah, same." Braden sighed. No matter how warm it was during the day, nights could still get chilly. Neither of them likely wanted to be stuck outside in their beach gear for too much longer.

As Monica gathered up her champagne and her

surfboard, Braden scooped sand over the fire. Almost immediately, the temperature plunged. Monica laughed as she shivered, and she looked over her shoulder in the direction of the parking lot.

"Be seeing you," she offered, turning back to Braden for a moment.

"Definitely," he agreed, offering her a grin. Her own smile was a bit more restrained, but honest all the same.

Braden watched her back as she walked away, a curious warmth building in his chest. He could try to tell himself that he was just glad she had gotten Connor out of her life, since he was apparently more of a scumbag than anyone had given him credit for. He knew the truth though. It seemed as if everyone in town thought there was something between them. Maybe he was beginning to hope that they were right.

CHAPTER TWELVE

In small towns, real estate could move pretty quickly. When Monica woke up on Wednesday morning, she had a message from Lori requesting they meet at the house that afternoon, and Monica already knew what it meant. Her offer had been accepted.

It was exciting, although not entirely surprising. The house had been on the market for quite some time, so the sellers had probably jumped at the offer as soon as they heard about it. It had been unoccupied and largely empty for just as long, so it wasn't as if the sellers needed to make any last stops at the house.

Monica texted Lori back, agreeing to meet her, before sitting down on her couch with a cup of coffee. She stared down at it as if it held all of the answers to any questions she had ever had or might ever have. Unfortunately for her, it continued to just be a cup of coffee.

It was exciting news. Monica knew that. But she couldn't help the way her thoughts began to trickle back toward Connor. They had been planning to do this together for so long, Monica supposed it was inevitable that she would think of him.

She had known he was growing distant, but cheating had never even occurred to her. She hadn't seen any signs of it on his social media. He always seemed to have convincing reasons for blowing Monica off when he missed calls or videos or trips.

She still wished that she had tried to press Naomi for more information during the phone call. Maybe she should try to call her back and get more details out of her.

Or maybe she should just call Connor and ask him directly. After all, who would have more accurate information than the source?

Once the idea was in her head, she couldn't get it out. She wasn't sure if it was a *good* idea. It barely even occurred to her that it wasn't even six o'clock on the other side of the country. One moment, the thought squirmed into her mind, and in the next moment, she was dialing his phone number. She wasn't even sure if she truly wanted him to answer or not.

"Monica?" Connor sounded slightly groggy when he answered the phone, but more than anything, he sounded about as confused as Monica had ever heard him sound. She realized it was very early where he was and, for a second, felt bad about waking him. Then she remembered what had inspired her call and stopped feeling bad. "What's going on?"

"I have a few questions," Monica replied, doing her absolute best to keep her voice as level as possible. "I think I deserve a few answers."

Connor sighed, long and slow. "Look, if you want her name so you can... I don't know, stalk her on social media or something—"

"I don't," Monica snapped, cutting him off. "And you know that. Of the two of us, only one of us is actively and purposefully cruel."

"Hey," Connor protested, "it's not like I deliberately set out to cheat."

"Oh, yeah, of course. I'm sure she just tripped into your arms and you blacked out and woke up with her in your bed." Monica scoffed. "Absolutely no intermediate steps where you could have, I don't know, reassessed what you were doing and made a choice not to do it."

"Come on—"

"Cheating doesn't happen on accident, Connor," Monica snapped. "You made a *choice* to do that. You can, at the *very least*, own the choice you made, and tell me why you made that *deliberate choice.*"

She could hear him grumbling, although she couldn't make out any of what he was saying. It probably wasn't particularly polite. Finally, he sighed and admitted, "I just couldn't see us having a life together anymore. I didn't want to go back to Whale Harbor, and I knew you didn't want to leave."

Monica waited for a moment, but when Connor didn't add anything else, a sharp, almost ugly laugh burst out of her and she asked, "That's it? You knew you didn't want to be with me, but it didn't occur to you to just tell me that until you had already been cheating on me for WEEKS? Come on, Connor. I know you have a better answer than that. If I was supposed to be your Plan B, you can just say that."

"I don't know," he huffed. "I just... didn't want to hurt you."

Monica rolled her eyes, and she was almost glad he wasn't actually there to see her. "Because I definitely wasn't hurt by you canceling on me at every opportunity. Great logic there."

She could hear some more grumbling, but he didn't make any further efforts to defend himself. Monica wasn't sure where she had wanted the conversation to go, but it was readily apparent it wasn't actually going anywhere.

"I never should have let you waste as much of my time as you did." Monica sighed, the fight and the anger seeming to seep out of her. "Hopefully she realizes you're a coward and you're cruel faster than I did, for her sake."

She could hear him taking a breath to say something—probably to try to defend himself—but she plowed onward before he could.

"Lose this number, please. I never want to hear from you again. You at least owe me that."

She hung up before he could get another word in. She didn't think he would try calling back—he had already made it clear he wanted nothing to do with her, after all—but she blocked his number regardless before dropping her phone onto the table.

She sat down in the nearest chair and slumped back into it, lifting her hands to cover her face. Truth be told, she wasn't even sure what she had been expecting that entire conversation to achieve. She didn't actually feel any better than she had five minutes ago.

Her thoughts kept spinning and churning. Were there signs she had missed? Should she have tried harder? Should she have not tried so hard? Had she done something wrong to push him into it? Logically, she knew the answer was no--there was never any excuse to cheat, no matter what--but she couldn't help thinking about it regardless. They had loved each other once. Why hadn't that fact been enough for him to give her the respect of cutting things off as soon as realized he wanted to? Why hadn't he just offered her that sliver of dignity?

Her thoughts spun so busily that she wasn't even sure of what she had been expecting or hoping for anymore.

She supposed she had been hoping she would get closure. Like she would have some realization about why it happened or what it meant, and she would suddenly understand it all and it would stop bothering her, and she could simply move on and leave it all behind her, where it belonged.

She felt no closure though. Instead, she was just angry and she felt like she might burst into tears at any moment. She chewed on her lip and held the tears at bay. She had cried enough over Connor. He didn't deserve more of her feelings. He didn't deserve more space in her thoughts than she had already given him.

What she needed was to get out of her house. Just sitting there staring at her ceiling wasn't helping anything.

She dumped what remained of her coffee into the sink, stepped into the first pair of shoes she found, and hurried out the door. Without putting much thought into it, she began to walk along the sidewalk with no plan or destination in mind, beyond seeing where her feet would take her.

No matter how hard she tried to hold the tears back, they were determined to come. When the first one fell, she gave up on trying to hold them back entirely, and let them silently slide down her cheeks as she walked. If nothing else, it meant the day probably wasn't going to get any worse.

* * *

Braden wasn't really planning to stop and have an in-depth conversation with anyone when he left the house. He walked to a doughnut shop near the house and bought a chocolate glazed doughnut, before he started walking toward the hardware store to do a couple price comparisons on a tool he needed for a project. As far as he was aware, it was going to be a fairly quiet day, assuming no one decided to bother him too much while he was working on renovations for one of his mother's friends—a big assumption, admittedly, since few people loved to talk more than friends of parents.

His doughnut was gone and he was halfway to the hardware store when he spotted Monica, a few yards ahead on the sidewalk and walking in the same direction. Even from behind her, he could tell something was wrong. Her arms were tightly crossed. Her shoulders were rounded. She was walking at more of a trudge, and her path seemed aimless, as if she was walking just to walk, rather than to get anywhere in particular.

Before he even realized it, Braden was picking up his pace to meet up with her.

He wasn't really sure if she would *want* to talk just then, but there was only one way to find out. He broke into a jog to catch up with her, and when he fell into step beside her, he wasn't surprised to see that she was crying. Even if it wasn't surprising, Braden felt a twinge in his chest. Monica deserved a world as bright and vibrant as she was. Hopefully, she would get to experience a world like that soon. It seemed as if every other time they saw each other, the world was trying to be the exact opposite.

She slid him a sidelong glance and made a halfhearted attempt at scrubbing her face with the back of one wrist. She gave the attempt up after a second and otherwise didn't bother trying to hide the evidence.

"Realized it's illegal to toss people into pits of cement?" Braden asked, shoving his hands into his pockets. It was stupid, but it was the first thing that occurred to him. Nevertheless, it had the desired effect. Monica laughed. It was short and a bit damp, but a laugh was a laugh.

Braden smiled at her cautiously, and the smile Monica offered in return was tiny and not particularly bright, but a win was a win.

"You know, if you want to talk about anything, I'm happy to listen," he said.

Monica nodded, and although her smile still wasn't as vibrant as Braden knew it could be, it did seem a bit more genuine.

"I know," she replied. "Just... maybe not right now."

Braden could work with that. Sometimes it was better to just walk with someone in silence.

CHAPTER THIRTEEN

It was approaching six o'clock on Wednesday evening, and Braden was heading to his mother's house. That in and of itself was nothing out of the ordinary. His mother loved having him over for dinner, and he loved being there. It was at least a weekly occurrence, and oftentimes even more than that.

However, when she had called him earlier to invite him, he had noted that she sounded way too excited about *just* inviting him over to dinner. He had tried to ask what was going on, and she had told him not to worry about it.

He supposed she had been successful on that front. He wasn't *worried* about it. After all, if his mother was *excited* about whatever her news was, then it couldn't be anything too grim. He was, however, so curious that it felt like his curiosity was going to chew a hole through the inside of his skull to escape, like one of those yappy little dogs slipping through a dog flap.

He let himself in like he usually did when he got to Gabrielle's house. He could hear her bustling around in the kitchen and smell dinner cooking.

"Come have a seat, dear!" Gabrielle called from the kitchen.

Obligingly, Braden toed his shoes off and wandered into the kitchen. Thomas was standing by the counter, keeping Gabrielle company as she worked her magic at the stove. That wasn't all that noteworthy. Thomas and Gabrielle both seemed happiest when they were within eyesight—and ideally arm's reach—of each other.

What *did* seem noteworthy was that the table had been covered with the good tablecloth from Nan, the table was set with the good jadeite dishware and the actual silverware, and there were candles in the middle of the table.

Braden's eyebrows rose slowly as he took in the sight. Dinner at his mother's house was usually a tidy affair, but this was certainly a few steps beyond the usual.

"Stop gawking at the table and sit down!" Gabrielle chided over her shoulder, and Braden dropped into his usual seat.

"Did you win the lottery?" he asked, baffled.

"Nothing like that," Gabrielle said, her green eyes dancing as she pulled the pan off the burner. Her graying brown hair was pulled back into a loose knot at the top of her neck.

"Did that one science teacher finally retire?" Braden asked instead.

Thomas politely cleared his throat behind one fist to mask a laugh as Gabrielle sighed with fond exasperation.

"Unfortunately not," she replied. "But it's good news all the same."

She didn't elaborate beyond that, instead moving on to moving dishes to the table. Evidently, she was very insistent on starting dinner first before she got to whatever news she wanted to share.

Soon though, all three of them were sitting around the table, and they all had food on their plates. At last, Gabrielle's patience seemed to wear out. She reached across the table to take Thomas's hand.

"We're getting married!" she burst out. She and

Thomas were both smiling so broadly their faces must ache.

Braden was quiet for a second as the information processed, and then a grin spread across his face. "Seriously?" he asked. "That's incredible! When did this happen?"

"Just a few days ago." Gabrielle sighed dreamily. "It was so romantic. He left a note in the book I was reading, and once I figured out what it meant, it led to a note in a different book, and then another book and another book, until I finally got to the last note in my favorite book, where he asked me to marry him."

"If I go into your room, am I going to find books on every surface?" Braden asked with a chuckle.

"You have no reason to go in my room right now," Gabrielle informed him primly. Braden took it as a yes.

From there, the conversation shifted to wedding ideas, although nothing was concrete yet. From the sounds of it, it was mostly just Gabrielle musing on potential ideas that might be nice, although Thomas offered his own suggestions too.

Ultimately, it sounded as if both of them would be happiest with a small wedding, with just the people closest to them in attendance. Something cozy and full of warmth.

Braden was sure the food was lovely, but as absorbed as he was by the excitement, he hardly tasted it. He waited until his mother excused herself to the bathroom before he looked at Thomas and said, "You know, I've never seen her this happy before."

"I hope I can keep making her happy," Thomas replied, sounding just a bit bashful as he said it.

"You will," Braden assured him. Back in D.C.—he was angrier back then, even if he still wasn't sure why—it might have come out as a playful threat. He would have meant well, but it would have carried an undercurrent of 'or else' all the same. Now though, it was just comfortably confident. He knew Thomas. He knew how much Thomas cared about—*loved*—Gabrielle. Thomas would keep making her happy. "And—" Braden wanted to say this before his mother came back, while it was just him and Thomas. Man to man. "I'm really happy to welcome you to the family. Officially, that is."

Thomas's smile was a little bit watery as he looked at Braden. "That really means a lot."

Gabrielle returned to the table before either of them could say anything else, and dinner continued from there, pleasant and lighthearted. Afterward, as

Braden headed home, it was probably inevitable that his thoughts turned toward romance.

Maybe he could imagine himself settling down and staying in Whale Harbor, as long as he wasn't alone. Maybe he could imagine himself finding the right woman. And maybe he already had a few feelings for one in particular.

Not that he was going to do anything about it right then. Monica was only just coming off of a heartbreak, and she had made it clear that she needed time to process and move on. Braden wasn't going to get in the way of that. At some point in the future, he would probably find a good time to ask her out, but not yet. He just had to wait until the right moment came up, whenever that moment might be.

The only issue was that he couldn't quite tell if he was being justifiably cautious about it, or if he was just too nervous to think about it too hard.

On Friday morning, Monica took an early lunch, left the library, and headed toward the docks, reaching them by around ten o'clock in the morning. She knew Braden's shifts on the fishing boat tended to end fairly early in the day, thanks to how early they started. She didn't have his schedule memorized, but she was hoping she would be able to catch him.

Part of her sort of wanted to apologize for the sorry state he caught her in the other day, but she knew that wouldn't go over well. He would never accept an apology for that, and she knew she didn't actually have anything to apologize for, even if she was still a little embarrassed. That wasn't the main reason she was there though.

The main reason Monica was there, pacing back and forth along one edge of the dock and watching the space she was positive the fishing boat usually wound up moored, was because she needed to talk to Braden about the new house—her B&B-to-be. The details of the sale were getting squared away faster than she ever would have hoped, so there was no sense in waiting to start making plans for the future of the house. The house needed some definite sprucing up, and she knew just the man for the job.

"Monica?"

A hand landed on Monica's shoulder and she nearly leapt out of her shoes with a yelp, whirling around to face Braden. She lifted a hand, pressing it flat to her chest over her heart.

"You nearly gave me a heart attack!"

Braden didn't look all that apologetic about it. In

fact, if Monica had to guess, she would say he looked like he was trying not to laugh at her. Looking past him, she could see the fishing boat, moored in a completely different area than she expected. She had simply failed to notice it. Maybe she deserved for him to laugh at her, just a little bit.

"What are you doing here?" Braden asked, mercifully not saying anything about how high she had jumped or the noise she had made.

"Looking for you," she replied. "I wanted to talk to you about the renovations to my new property."

Braden straightened up, seeming to go into business mode in an instant. He folded his arms over his chest. "What did you have in mind?"

"Like I mentioned before, it's mostly a lot of modernizing and landscaping, although I'll call in a specialist to handle the landscaping, and I want some shelving units added," she said. "Actual shelving units. No Ikea chic. I want to know that if I put an antique typewriter on the shelf, it's not going to wind up broken on the floor in a week."

"Do you even have an antique typewriter?" Braden asked her wryly.

"You never know what the future may hold," Monica replied, before waving the topic off. "The biggest thing is that I want a front porch. Something comfortable with a decent view of the sunset, I think." Monica gave him her most winning smile as she asked, "Do you think you could make that happen?"

She probably didn't even need to try particularly hard to win him over, as he started thinking it over immediately.

Distracted, Braden started pacing, and as he turned his back toward Monica, she couldn't help but to notice the outline of his shoulders through his t-shirt. Had he always had shoulders like that? How had she never noticed before?

She shook her head slightly, dragging her thoughts back to the topic at hand. It was one thing to notice Braden's smile, but his shoulders? She was just coming off a breakup. She shouldn't be thinking about anyone like that... should she? Not now, she thought as Braden paced back toward her. Luckily, he was so caught up in whatever he was pondering for the deck that he didn't seem to have noticed her moment of distraction.

"This wouldn't be the first deck I've built, so I'm not worried about that," he said, sounding slightly distracted. "As long as you don't want anything huge, it shouldn't be an issue."

"Nothing huge," Monica said reassuringly. "I

don't want it to look out of place with the house. I just want there to be more options for relaxing outside, other than the back patio."

"It should be pretty doable," Braden said, nodding along almost absentmindedly. Monica was pretty sure he was still thinking about how to make the deck work, but before she could say anything, something caught her attention.

Behind Braden, back at the fishing boat, one of the crew members was waving his arms over his head, trying to get Braden's attention, or to get Monica's attention to then get Braden's attention. He didn't seem panicked or urgent, but the look on his face said that he had been trying to flag Braden down for at least a couple of minutes.

"Um..." Monica trailed off, lifting a hand and pointing a finger over Braden's shoulder. "I think you have a situation back there."

Braden turned to look over his shoulder, and he heaved a sigh as he turned away. Before he started walking, he glanced back at Monica and said, "Give me a call when you want me to come take a look at the house, so I can give you a price estimate. All right?"

"Will do. I'll give you a call once all of the paperwork is squared away." Monica nodded once, smiling crookedly. "Now shoo." She waved him off, smiling.

As Braden hurried back toward the fishing boat to see what they needed him for, Monica watched him go for a moment before turning to leave. There was a pleasant warmth settling in her gut.

She supposed she could tell herself it was because she was excited to be making progress on the bed and breakfast. And that was certainly part of it, although she knew that wasn't the whole story. For the time being though, telling herself that was enough. She could look at the rest of the picture later, and for the moment, she could just appreciate the steps forward she was making toward her dream.

CHAPTER FOURTEEN

Marty got to Darla and Rick's house right around dinner time, and she could see Monica's car already parked outside. Marty had been hoping for a moment alone with Darla, but she supposed there was nothing for it now. She had been hoping to discuss her current job crisis with her sister in private first, just for her own comfort. After all, whatever decision she made for her job would also impact how much she got to see her family in the future.

If she left Whale Harbor, she would be leaving Darla behind. They had already gone for years where they barely saw each other when Darla lived in New York. Marty didn't want to go back to living like that. She didn't want to give up the option of marrying Wyatt, having a home, and starting a family. She didn't want to lose the family she already had.

As Marty approached the front door, she pushed those thoughts out of her mind. It felt as if it had been eighteen years since the last time they had a girls' night, and she didn't want to ruin it by going into it in a bad mood.

When Marty stepped inside, Darla greeted her with an excited, "There you are!" and pressed a glass of wine into her hand before pulling her into the living room, forcing Marty to awkwardly step out of her shoes on the way. The start menu for *Legally Blonde* was on the television screen, the menu music looping endlessly, and the coffee table and one of the end tables were covered in various types of chips and baked goods.

"Were you expecting to feed an army?" Marty asked, taking in the spread as she took a seat on the couch. Monica was sitting on the other end of the couch, already halfway through a chocolate croissant.

"I got a bit excited," Darla said, shrugging sheepishly. "Everything looked good, so I just... got a bit of everything."

"And she broke out the good stuff," Monica

added, holding up her wine glass by the stem, before lowering it and taking a sip.

"I'm sure we're both honored," Marty replied.

Darla hit play on the movie and dropped down into the armchair. She stretched her arms over her head and sagged back into the chair, before finally looking at Monica. It was as if the movie didn't even exist, but that was par for the course during these kinds of nights.

"Sooo... ?" Darla asked, drawing the word out slowly.

"Sooo... what?" Monica asked, with just a hint of a sly smile on her face.

Darla rolled her eyes. "So, tell us what's going on with the new house!"

"Nothing, right now!" Monica replied. "The paperwork is happening fast, but it isn't happening *that* fast!"

"But you have to have ideas," Marty said, before finally taking a sip of her wine. "What are you thinking?"

"Right now, I'm mostly figuring out what sort of renovations will need to be done," Monica said. "I talked to Braden about it, so hopefully I'll have an idea of the price soon-ish."

Marty slid a glance toward Darla, catching her eye. Her eyebrows rose, and Darla grinned.

"And that's all you've been talking to Braden about?" Darla asked, trying to sound innocent and mostly missing the mark.

"Not entirely," Monica replied cautiously. "We've talked about a lot of things."

Marty and Darla shared another look.

"What kinds of things?" Marty asked.

Monica pointed one finger at Marty. "Don't." She swung her finger to put in Darla's direction. "And don't. I know what you're both trying to get at."

Darla blinked, her most guileless and earnest look on her face. "And what might that be?"

"I'm still in the middle of getting over Connor and that entire mess," Monica pointed out. "I haven't even begun to think about dating anyone else."

"Dating? Who said anything about dating? You're the one who brought up dating," Darla replied in a too-innocent singsong.

"But since you *did* bring it up," Marty added, "what *do* you two talk about?"

"All sorts of things," Monica replied, evasive at first, but then thoughtful as she said, "He's actually really easy to talk to." She leaned against the arm of the couch and propped her chin up on her free hand.

"He even got me to laugh after my last chat with Connor. I don't think he even knew what was wrong. He just knew that I was upset."

"That's not nothing," Darla said as if it was some sort of reminder, gesturing at Monica with a potato chip before popping it into her mouth.

"You shouldn't discount that sort of thing!" Marty said, stretching her leg across the couch to prod Monica in the knee with her foot. "For a lot of people, it takes ages to find that."

"I know, I know." Monica shooed Marty's foot away before mumbling, "And I guess it sort of feels like I've been single for a while already."

Marty and Darla shared a look again.

"Stop that." Monica huffed at them. "Just because *you two* like to think you're psychic doesn't mean all of us do."

"We didn't even do anything," Darla replied, still attempting to play innocent. "What was it you were saying?"

"You heard me." Monica heaved a sigh and took a long sip of her wine. "It's not like I saw or even talked to Connor every day. He was barely in my life. It feels like I've already been single for years."

"That might be for the best," Marty replied carefully. She didn't want to go tromping all over

Monica's feelings, of course, but she also didn't think Connor deserved to have that much real estate in Monica's feelings. It wouldn't be so terrible if he turned into a foot note sooner rather than later.

"Maybe," Monica replied, before straightening up and looking at Darla. "But what about you?" she asked. "My relationship—or lack thereof—isn't the only one that's going through some changes."

"We did finally get to start with the actual wedding planning," Darla said, and she sounded relieved more than anything. "I swear, it took half an eon before we could just sit down and talk without something coming up, but once we could, it seemed easy. We're more or less on the same page as each other. We might even have a venue picked out, although I suppose it will depend on availability." Her smile as she spoke was almost secretive.

"Well?" Marty prompted her after a moment. "You can't just say that and then not give us any details!"

"I don't want to get ahead of myself! We're still at the point where anything could happen or any details could change, for any reason!"

Marty threw a throw pillow at her. Given the name, it seemed appropriate. Laughing, Darla caught it and hugged it to her chest.

"All right, fine. We're thinking about that estate just outside of town. The one on the beach."

Monica gasped and cried, "Oh, that will be perfect!" Her mind was already racing with design possibilities, but she vowed to keep her mouth shut unless Darla asked for help. She didn't want to overstep.

"That's the idea," Darla said wryly, before turning her attention to Marty. "What about you? Have you and Wyatt thought about it at all?"

Marty shifted in her seat, fidgeting uncomfortably for a moment before saying, "We're actually having a bit of an issue right now." She hated her phrasing as soon as the words left her mouth, but she wasn't sure how else to say it.

Darla straightened up in her seat, letting the pillow fall to the floor as she did. Her expression grew serious. "What's going on?"

"It's nothing that serious," Marty hurried to reply. "Just... I got a job offer, but it's in San Francisco. I've been waffling back and forth on what to do about it, but I'm running out of time. I have to decide by tomorrow whether I want to accept the interview."

"So, what's the hold up?" Monica asked. "There shouldn't be any harm in just giving it a try. Going for an interview isn't the same thing as a commitment?"

"But what if I go to San Francisco and it turns out I *like* it?" Marty asked. "Wyatt can't go with me, if that's the case. He has a business and a life here. And..." Marty trailed off, suddenly feeling terrible about what she had been about to say. But Darla and Monica were both looking at her expectantly, so she picked her train of thought back up. "And, well... we know how badly long-distance relationships can go."

"That's true," Monica said, agreeing slowly, "but it doesn't *have* to be. I mean, things with me and Connor went south for a whole host of reasons. The distance was, honestly, probably the least of them." She shrugged almost casually as she admitted it. "A long-distance relationship is going to work as well as the people in the relationship are willing to make it work. A strong, committed couple will be just fine."

"I know, I know." Marty sighed. "It's just a lot to think about."

She didn't protest when the conversation turned toward lighter topics, the movie continuing to play in the background. She knew they were right, and it sparked a flicker of hope in her chest as she thought about it, but she still couldn't completely squash the pit of dread building right beside that bit of hope.

She knew she had a lot she needed to think about before tomorrow, but it could wait until she was back home again. For now, she settled more comfortably into the couch, sipped her wine, and let the conversation wash over her.

It was nearly ten o'clock when Wyatt heard Marty get home that night. He heard the front door squeak open and then quietly thump closed, and he heard the sound of her shoes on the floor.

"Did you have a good time?" he asked, projecting his voice to be heard from the en suite bathroom. Considering he was in the middle of brushing his teeth, it came out sounding more like *Di' 'ou haf'a goo' ti'?*

He could hear Marty's footsteps moving into the bedroom, and she poked her head around the bathroom door frame a moment later.

"I did," she said, smiling quietly. She had shed her coat already, and she tugged a few clips out of her curly dark brown hair, stepping into the bathroom and setting them in a small container on a shelf.

Wyatt waited until he had spit out the toothpaste

and rinsed his mouth before saying, "Good to hear. How's Monica holding up?"

"She seems to be doing all right." Marty wrinkled her nose a bit as she shrugged. "As well as can be expected, at any rate, and that's all anyone can really ask for."

"And your sister?" Wyatt asked.

"She and Rick are finally starting their wedding planning!" Marty said as the two of them stepped out of the bathroom and sat on the bed. "I guess they finally found some time to sit down and really talk about it. Or, knowing Darla, she grabbed a chunk of time with both fists and told it that it was staying put if it knew what was good for it."

'*And what about us?*' Wyatt wanted to ask, spurred on by the mention of wedding planning, but he also didn't want to drag down the mood. So instead, he settled on saying, "Good for them. Hopefully they won't run into any other complications."

Marty nodded, and for a moment, the two of them sat in silence. She rested her head on his shoulder, slipping her hand into his as Trouble padded into the room, purring softly. The cat jumped up onto the bed beside them, and Marty used her free hand to give the furry feline a loving scratch. It all felt so comfortable and domestic that it made a pleasant ache swell in Wyatt's chest.

He turned his head a little, pressing a kiss to Marty's hair and inhaling the familiar scent of her shampoo.

"You know I love you, right?" he asked, his voice muffled by her soft, dark curls.

Marty lifted her head to look at him, her eyebrows rising. "Of course I do! Why would you even ask me that?"

The warmth of the room and the soft sound of Trouble's purring made it feel like they were in their own cozy little bubble. It made Wyatt feel brave enough to say, "I want what's best for you, Mar. But I'm worried about what will happen to us if you take that job in San Francisco."

She sucked in a breath, and he could see the tears that sprang to her eyes. He felt terrible making her feel bad, but they had to talk about this.

"I think..." She spoke hesitantly. "I think I want to take the interview. I don't know if I'll take the job even if I get it, but I think if I don't at least see what's out there, I'll regret it."

Wyatt's heart sank a little, but he nodded, determined to support her. "I understand."

Marty was such a talented designer, and it was

impossible not to love her personality. He had no doubt that she would be offered the job. He also didn't blame her for being curious about life outside Whale Harbor. He had left the town himself once, after all, seeking out bigger adventures and experiences. But Wyatt was a changed man, and he knew now what was most important to him.

"Mar," he said seriously, looking down into her eyes. "If this job is your dream—if you need to go, I'll sell the shop. I'll go with you."

She gasped. "I would never ask you to do that!"

He smiled. His sweet thoughtful Marty. "You didn't ask. I offered. Besides, I can sell quads anywhere. None of that matters to me half as much as you do."

She sighed dreamily and tilted her face up for a kiss. "I am the luckiest girl in the world, huh? What did I ever do to deserve you?"

"That's my line," he teased, giving her a sweet kiss.

Then Marty's mouth twisted ruefully. "Your dad would kill me if you sold the shop on my account."

"Nah." Wyatt shook his head. "He'd just buy it from me and then brag about expanding his empire. Although..." He gave her a jokingly shy look. "He'd probably insist you make an honest man out of me if you dragged me all the way across the country to be with you."

Marty laughed heartily. "Oh, would he?"

"My honor is at stake."

She laughed again, then grew serious. "It means everything to me that you're willing to work so hard to make sure we stay together," she said, giving him a soft smile.

"*You* mean everything to me," Wyatt replied.

She wiped at her eyes. "I'm not crying. It's just allergies."

"You don't have allergies," he pointed out, chuckling.

Marty gave him a playful shove. "Oh hush, you. Never mind that. Just kiss me." She threw her arms around his neck.

Wyatt pulled the love of his life into his arms and did as she commanded.

CHAPTER FIFTEEN

Monica looked around and resisted the urge to giggle like a little kid. Her bid had been accepted. The B&B was all hers! Lori had called her that morning with the good news, and Monica had rushed over to the building, wondering if it would look even more perfect now that it was actually hers.

It definitely did, she thought as she looked around, a goofy smile on her face.

She was still wearing that grin when Braden walked in a little while later, startling her out of her thoughts.

"Oh, hi!" Monica said, resisting the urge to put a hand to her hair to make sure it wasn't too messy. She'd rushed out of the house with barely a glance in the mirror. Then she shook her head at herself inwardly. She was being silly. Braden had seen her in all sorts of states, including when she'd had salt-crusted hair after an afternoon of surfing, and he still liked her. Still, she supposed it wasn't unreasonable to want to look her best when faced with the man she was starting to have a serious crush on.

"Hi," Braden said. "I wondered if I was going to find you here. I heard the sale went through and I wanted to look the place over, now that it's official."

She shook her head. "Whale Harbor gossip mill, huh?"

"Faster than the telephone," he agreed with a laugh. "Anyway, I'd still love to help with the remodel if you'd still like to have me."

"Oh, absolutely! Let me tell you what I'm thinking!"

She launched into a description of her vision, starting with the front room where they stood. She pointed to the walls where she wanted floor-to-ceiling bookshelves, possibly with some of those old-fashioned rolling ladders attached for assistance reaching the high shelves. The room had hardwood floors, which she wanted to preserve. They would need refinishing and she would have to get some cozy area rugs to keep the chill away from guests' feet in the winter. She and Braden turned in place as she talked, until they were facing the large bay windows, through which they could see the large, lovely porch.

"I can't decide if I want to paint it something neutral, like a nice gray, or something vibrant and eye-catching, like a pretty teal. The first choice would be more classic, but the second would grab people's attention, which maybe would help lure in passersby who were looking for lodging in the area, instead of just people who looked us up beforehand."

Out of the corner of her eye, Monica caught sight of Braden nodding thoughtfully. Suddenly, she realized she had been talking for a *long* time—and he had been quiet throughout her speech.

"Oh my goodness," she said, blushing a little. "I'm so sorry. I've been talking forever."

He grinned at her. "Don't apologize. The architect in me loves hearing about plans for buildings. And besides, your ideas sound incredible. I would love to stay here if I were visiting Whale Harbor."

Monica paused, wondering if what she was about to ask was any of her business. Then her curiosity got the best of her. "Will you be visiting Whale Harbor? Or is your stay here going to be permanent?" She added in a joke to soften her nosiness. "I know we have *way* more nightlife and excitement than boring old Washington D.C., but maybe you're missing it for other reasons."

Braden gave her a smile before his expression turned thoughtful. "I'm not sure," he admitted. "For a while, I was certain I would never want to stay. But I'm definitely happy here for now. And I'll want to stick around for my mom's wedding—did you hear she and Thomas got engaged?"

"No!" Had she just been praising the efficiency of the Whale Harbor gossip mill? She took it all back. "That's so exciting."

"It is," he agreed. "Thomas made this big romantic gesture. He hid notes in my mom's favorite books, one clue leading her to the next, until she found the big question in her number one favorite."

"That's adorable." Monica was happy for the older couple. They'd both gone through a lot, losing their spouses, and it made her feel hopeful to watch them find love again. She would never compare her breakup to surviving the death of a loved one, of course, but even just the idea that people got second chances made her feel optimistic.

Your second chance could be standing right in front of you, said a voice in her mind that sounded a lot like Darla and Marty.

"They're pretty cute together," Braden admitted.

"It's funny, because I was so suspicious of Thomas at first—which is crazy, because my mom is amazing, so it makes sense that he would notice that."

"You were just being protective of your mom." Monica nudged him with her shoulder. "That's pretty cute too, you know."

He nudged her back. "Oh, stop. The thing is, I'm not just glad Thomas is marrying my mom for her sake, although she's obviously over the moon about it. I'm happy for me too. I love how much we all get along."

Monica glanced up at him. He was wearing his usual fisherman's hat and had a tiny bit of stubble growing that suggested that he hadn't shaved this morning. "It's a good town," she said, trying not to admire how nice he looked, even on a regular Wednesday morning. "You fit in well here."

He lowered his chin to look at her and she couldn't help but think what it would feel like to kiss him. He was such a sweet, kind man—would his kisses be soft and gentle? But he was also sturdy and dependable, so maybe he would kiss confidently, like a man who knew what he was doing. She was almost tempted to push up onto her tiptoes and find out as their eyes met and held.

At the last minute though, she chickened out,

turning to look out the window of her new building, instead. She couldn't risk her heart on a man who might head off to the big city, not after Connor and not now that purchasing the B&B meant her life was even more firmly tied to Whale Harbor than it had been before.

The spell between them broke as she looked away, and Monica worried for a minute that things would be awkward. She didn't need to be afraid. Things were never awkward between her and Braden, and he wasn't the kind of person who would get annoyed at someone for not pushing further than they wanted to.

"Have you been doing much surfing recently?" he asked after a moment.

"Sadly no." She risked a glance at him. He looked like his normal friendly self and she relaxed. Maybe she wasn't ready to take the risk of asking him out right now, but she wasn't sure she wanted the door to get closed on any possibility of more between them either. And she certainly wanted to be his friend, no matter whether things ever turned romantic. "I've been so busy learning what it takes to run a business that I haven't had time. And now that I've actually bought the place, I'm afraid I'll have even less time."

"You should make time!" Braden playfully put his hands on his hips. "Unless all that talk about how you're a great surfer is just that—talk."

Monica mimicked his pose. "Is that a challenge?"

"You bet it is."

She laughed. So much of her time with Connor had been spent worrying that she had forgotten how great it was just to have easy fun with a man. "You're on, Watson. Name the time and place."

He stuck out his hand to shake. "Let's say Saturday, if you're not working. I'll check the tide schedule and text you what time."

She stuck her hand in his and shook on it. "It's a plan."

* * *

Wyatt tried not to show how nervous he was feeling as he drove Marty to the airport. It wasn't that he didn't trust Marty—he trusted her with his life and, maybe more importantly, his heart. But he didn't like this feeling of everything being so up in the air.

To distract himself, he made cheerful conversation. "Okay, so you have to send me pictures of every cool thing you do, okay?"

"Okay!" She laughed. It maybe wasn't Wyatt's

first time making this request. "Ghirardelli Square, the Golden Gate Bridge, the pastel houses—anything else you want me to visit for you?"

"Don't forget to take a trolley car!"

She pretended to make a note on an invisible notepad. "You got it, boss."

They talked about other lighthearted topics as they drove, keeping away from the one thing that Wyatt knew worried them both: that their lives were about to change. He regaled her with a story of a customer who had asked if the quads Wyatt sold had to have four wheels.

"I never actually figured out if he wanted more wheels or fewer," he said as Marty gasped with laughter. "All I could think of to say was, 'You know why they're called quads, right?'"

"Why is there always one customer who wants the impossible?" She wiped away tears of mirth. "Where would the other wheels even *go* on a quad? Or would that make it a quint?"

"Who knows!"

As they got closer to the airport, Marty grew quieter and quieter and by the time they pulled up to the departures area, she was gnawing at her bottom lip anxiously.

"Hey." Wyatt put his hand on Marty's knee,

which was bouncing up and down. "Are you sure you don't want me to go in with you? I can't go through security, but I could wait with you a little while longer."

She shook her head. "No, I think I'm just going to buy a cup of tea and sip it at my gate until I feel a little calmer." She waved her hands around her head. "This whole thing is just so crazy."

He squeezed her knee. "This is just an exploratory trip, remember? So try and treat the whole thing like an adventure. If you love it and want to live there for the rest of our lives, we'll figure it out. If you realize you can't live without a decent lobster roll and need to come back here, that's great too. But until we know more, try to have some fun, okay? And either way, you know I'm in your corner."

She leaned over and gave him a lingering kiss. "You're the best, do you know that?"

"I'm pretty great," he said with a laugh. "Now, let's get you going, huh?"

They both got out of the car, and Wyatt helped Marty with her bag. Before she turned to go into the airport, she wrapped her arms around him in a fierce hug.

"You do what you need to do, and I'll be right

here waiting for you," he said, pressing his cheek against the top of her head.

"I love you," Marty said.

"I love you too."

They hugged for a few seconds more, then Marty broke off to head inside. Wyatt watched, leaning against the trunk of his car, as she went to the check-in desk, already looking more excited. After she finished at the desk, she turned and waved to him through the glass doors before heading deeper into the airport.

Wyatt watched her go, feeling like he was watching his heart walk away with her. With a sigh, he got back behind the wheel of his car, already counting the hours until she was back again.

CHAPTER SIXTEEN

Braden lay awake in bed, staring at his ceiling. It wasn't late by most people's standards—just after ten o'clock at night—but Braden was a man who got up before the sun. This was basically the middle of the night for him.

He rolled over with a huff, hoping he'd have more luck sleeping on his side. Except getting comfortable wasn't the problem. The problem was that he couldn't stop thinking about Monica.

He tried not to judge other people, especially people he didn't know, but he couldn't help but think that Monica's ex was a jerk and an idiot. What kind of man would string along a woman by letting her think they had a future together, when he knew he had no intention of living the sort of life that would work for them both? Even though he didn't know what this Connor guy looked like, Braden briefly indulged in a highly satisfying fantasy of 'accidentally' dumping a bucket of fish guts on the guy if he ever came to town. Braden had suffered that fate—though in his case it had been an actual accident, not a pretend one—once or twice while he was learning the fishing business, so he knew it was not a nice experience.

As fun as it was to imagine some fancy city boy hopping around in outrage as his expensive shoes got ruined, it didn't help him sleep. After a few more minutes of tossing and turning, he had to admit to himself that this was because the person he was really annoyed with wasn't Connor—it was himself.

Monica didn't deserve to be pursued by someone else who wasn't sure he was going to stick around, so even though his feelings were starting to move out of the 'crush' territory and into a world where he could really see them building something together, he knew he needed to be sure of himself before he made a move. He wouldn't be able to live with himself if he hurt her just because he was careless.

A few minutes later, in which sleep didn't get any closer, Braden hauled himself out of bed with a huff. If he wasn't going to manage to fall asleep, and that felt like it wasn't going to be happening any time soon, he might as well accomplish something rather than just let his mind race pointlessly all night. He quickly got dressed, deciding to head over to the B&B. He planned to get started on work the next day, but one more look around would help him decide what order to do things. And if the place reminded him of Monica? *That was an added bonus,* he thought to himself.

Despite Monica's joke about Whale Harbor nightlife the previous day, the streets were quiet as Braden drove over to the B&B. He pulled into the driveway and got out of the car, admiring how the stately old house looked in the glow of the streetlamps. It really was the perfect place for the kind of business that Monica wanted to open. The peaceful ambiance of the place made him want to curl up with a paperback and a mug of tea, possibly with a dollop of whiskey in it to make a hot toddy, if he was feeling particularly festive. And that was how he felt before any of the repair work had been done. He could scarcely imagine how good the place would look once it had fresh paint, updated appliances, and all the bookshelves that Monica could ever dream of.

Braden walked up the front steps, running his hand along the railing, considering how he would build the porch Monica envisioned. He thought about her color dilemma and wondered if she'd be interested in keeping the porch a muted shade but adding some bright blue Adirondack chairs for a pop of color. He could make those for her too, if she wanted. That would be the best of both worlds.

Lost in architectural musings, Braden used the key Monica had given him to let himself in through the front door. He headed for the kitchen—as much as the porch project excited him, ripping out tile and reworking electrical and water lines was messy work, so it was probably best to start there. Braden was mentally running through a list of demo crews who might be willing to take on work in Whale Harbor when he heard a sound. He froze. Had someone broken in? It was widely known around town that the house was currently unoccupied, so there was some risk.

Quietly, he crept back toward the living room. He heard the sound again—footsteps.

His hand was already reaching out to flick on the living room light when he heard someone call, "Who's there?"

He recognized that voice, but it was too late. Light was already flooding the room.

Monica let out a little shriek of surprise and

whirled around, brandishing a can of pepper spray at him.

Braden threw both his hands up in the air. "It's just me! Don't shoot!" He didn't even care if that sounded silly and dramatic. Maybe it would serve him right for startling a woman alone at night, but still, he *really* didn't want to get pepper sprayed.

Fortunately, Monica's reflexes were fast. "Oh my gosh." She laughed, dropping the hand holding the spray and pressing the other to her chest. "Braden. You scared me half to death!"

Braden rubbed the back of his neck ruefully. "Sorry about that." When he'd been home, lying awake in bed, coming here had seemed like a good idea. Now... he wasn't so sure.

She didn't seem mad though. Now that her fright had passed, she looked happy to see him. "Boy, am I glad you weren't an intruder. I've carried that pepper spray for years as a safety precaution, but I hope I never have to use it. What are you doing here so late at night, anyway?"

"I couldn't sleep," he admitted. "I thought I would get a look at things before I get started tomorrow."

"Funny, I couldn't sleep either, so I came over

here to prepare the walls for the wallpaper I want to put up. Great minds think alike, huh?"

"Definitely," he agreed. "What's this wallpaper?"

Monica's eyes lit with excitement. "Ooh, it's amazing. Come see!" She beckoned him into the front room. The rolls of wallpaper were stacked neatly up against the fireplace, but one was laid out so she could admire it. He bent closer to look. Was that... ?

"It's book quotes," she told him happily. "It'll be a huge challenge to get the edges to match up, but the end result will be so amazing that I think it will be worth it."

That was perfect for this place. Braden grinned at her, delighted by her happiness. "It will definitely be worth it."

He glanced around. There was a faint layer of dust from where Monica had been sanding the walls. She'd obviously been here for a while. "How did I not see your car when I got here?"

She looked up from where she was still gazing happily down at the wallpaper. "Oh, I parked around the back. Did you come in from the front?"

"Yeah." He looked around again. "Are you wrapping up here or keeping going?"

"I think I'll keep going," she said. "I know it's late

and this is a big project and maybe I should pace myself, but I just couldn't resist getting started."

Her excitement was infectious. "You're really passionate about this whole thing," he told her. "It's really amazing."

"Thanks." Monica's expression grew serious—though not sad, Braden was glad to note. "You know, I started this as a distraction from the breakup with Connor. Maybe that sounds weird, because originally this was going to be something we did together. But seizing this opportunity felt like a way to take the breakup and make something good out of it, now that I didn't have a reason to wait." She paused thoughtfully. "But it's more than that, now. It's not just a distraction or a silver lining—it's my next chapter."

"That's amazing," Braden repeated. "You're amazing." He hesitated, not sure if he should say this next bit, then decided that maybe she needed to hear it. "And, if you ask me, Connor is an idiot for letting you go."

She looked up at him, a pretty blush spreading across her cheeks. They were standing close to one another, and it occurred to him that this would be a perfect moment to kiss her, alone in this beautiful house with this wonderful, determined, resilient woman. He really wanted to. But he wasn't sure about his plans yet, and he couldn't lead her on, so he didn't.

That didn't stop, him, however, from looking his fill, taking in her dancing green eyes and happy expression as he thought about how sometimes it was really hard to do the right thing.

Monica's heart was hammering so hard she felt like it would break right through her chest. For a second there she had been so sure that Braden was going to lean in and kiss her—and, crazily enough, she was disappointed that he hadn't.

Was it really crazy though? Sure, her breakup was still pretty recent, but she didn't need more time to know that Braden was nothing like Connor. She thought back to what Darla and Marty had told her —when it was the right person, it didn't matter how much time it had been since your last relationship, or what speed you were 'supposed to' go. With the right person, everything fell into place.

That thought almost gave her enough courage to reach up and kiss him herself—almost, but not quite.

She found she was brave enough to reach out and squeeze his hand quickly.

"Thank you," she said. "It means a lot to hear you say that."

He squeezed back. "People should always say nice things to you, Mon. You don't have to thank me for it."

His hand was warm and had rough calluses on them—that made sense, she thought, given that he was part fisherman, part contractor. The roughness was nice though. Maybe even a little too nice, she realized, as a giddy feeling rose in the pit of her stomach. She made herself let his hand go before she let it go too much to her head.

The movement broke the spell between them, and Braden moved away a little, then turned so they both were facing the wall where Monica had been working before she'd heard the 'intruder.'

"Want some help with this?" He waved a hand at the expanse of wall that still needed to be sanded flat before the wallpaper could be applied.

She glanced at her watch. It was almost eleven at night and she knew he had to be up early. "Are you sure?" Her tone was doubtful.

"Positive. I'm up at night pretty regularly,

unfortunately. My brain just sometimes doesn't want to quiet down."

She could commiserate. "Isn't insomnia the worst?"

"You too?" he asked. "How do you deal with it?"

"Nighttime walks on the beach, usually." Monica walked over to her box of supplies and took out some extra sanding pads, handing one to Braden. "It's peaceful and quiet and the ocean is so vast that it makes my problems seem insignificant in comparison. How about you?"

He took the pad and got right to work. "I'm really into mystery novels, actually. Maybe I'll have to come read one at this new B&B I hear is opening. It has a book theme, you should check it out."

She laughed at his joke. "Mystery novels though? That's a terrible choice."

He looked shocked. "Don't tell me you're a snob about mysteries!"

Monica stopped sanding to put her hands on her hips. "I'm a librarian, Braden. I love all books. No—I just meant that mysteries are a terrible choice if you're trying to go to sleep. Either it will be scary or it will make you want to know what happens next—and neither of those are good for sleep!"

Braden nodded like he'd never thought of that.

"Wow, that's a good point. What's the best late-night read, in your professional opinion?"

"Romance novels," she said at once. "You know everyone will end up happy, so you don't have to worry. Or something really boring—that works too."

"You are the expert," he said. "I'll have to try that. Although, next time you're up late, you should give me a call. If I'm up too, we can go for a walk together." He was watching her out of the corner of his eye and Monica thought he might be flirting with her.

Her heart started racing again. "I'll do that," she said, trying to sound casual.

They finished the small patch of wall they were working on, and she put her sander back in the box. Insomnia or no, she was starting to get pretty tired. "I think that's about all I've got in me for tonight."

Braden stepped back to look at their work. "We made good progress, but you're right. This is a good stopping point."

They packed up their supplies quickly and headed outside. Braden insisted on walking Monica to her car. Even though it was a safe area, it was late. "You don't even want to have to use that pepper spray, remember?" he joked.

He stood next to her car as she climbed into the

driver's seat. "Don't forget," he reminded her before she closed the door. "Surfing Saturday."

She smiled. "I'm looking forward to it."

And as she pulled away, Braden raising a hand in farewell as she took off, Monica realized just how true that was.

CHAPTER SEVENTEEN

Marty stood in her hotel room in San Francisco and looked at the entire contents of her suitcase, which she'd strewn out on her bed. Her attire at *Sand 'n' Things* was professional, but definitely on the more casual end of things, so she wasn't accustomed to dressing for a big corporation. Back home in Whale Harbor, she hadn't known what to wear, so she'd packed every item of business clothing she owned, thinking she would make the final decision about her outfit when it was time for the interview.

Well, it was almost time for the interview—a glance at the clock told her she had an hour left—and she still didn't know what to wear.

"Okay," she said out loud, hoping the pep talk would motivate her. "Let's make some choices."

First step: skirt or trousers? Skirt, she decided. Of the three that she'd brought, her favorite was a black pencil skirt that always made her feel powerful. She set that aside.

Next: which shirt should she wear? Two of her options didn't go with the skirt, so she cast those aside. She was left with a light blue cotton button down and a white silk blouse. She held each choice up in front of the mirror, swapping back and forth a few times before deciding on the white. The silk made her look mature, professional, accomplished. That was exactly the impression she wanted to give.

Marty put on the skirt and blouse and looked at her reflection. She looked good, but the plain black and white was too austere. And her interview was at a design firm, after all! She pulled a silk scarf with a pink and white floral pattern out of her pile of accessories and arranged it jauntily around her neck, then stepped into her heels. There. That looked perfect. Or did it?

With a sigh at her own indecisiveness, Marty shimmied out of the skirt and swapped in a slate gray pair of trousers. Okay. *That* looked perfect.

She was giving the outfit a final once-over, feeling pleased with the result, when her phone buzzed on the bedspread, indicating a text.

WYATT: Good luck today, sweetheart!!! You've got this. It's impossible not to love you!

For a second, she pressed her phone to her chest, overcome with love for him. Wyatt didn't even want her to come here, and yet he still remembered when her interview was happening and made sure to send her such a loving, supportive text beforehand.

If she was being honest with herself, receiving this text made Marty feel a pang of doubt. Not about Wyatt, of course—he was everything she'd ever wanted: a wonderful, sweet man who loved Whale Harbor as much as she did. And he was her best friend on top of that! No, what she doubted was what she was even doing coming out to California for this interview. After a lifetime in Whale Harbor, she had found San Francisco a little bit overwhelming. It had been fun to play the tourist these last few days—and to send all her pictures to Wyatt, of course—but the whole time, there had been a little voice at the back of her head that wondered if she could ever really be happy here.

She took a deep breath and remembered Wyatt's words from when he dropped her off. This was a fact-finding mission. She didn't have to make any decisions yet. Encouraged by this thought, she looked at her phone to return his message.

MARTY: Thanks! *heart emoji* I'm pretty nervous!

WYATT: Psh, I'm not. THEY should be nervous. They aren't gonna know what hit 'em.

Marty sent back a string of heart emojis and then told him she would call after her interview to give him the scoop on everything. Then it was time to call her rideshare, who pinged her that they were downstairs only a few minutes later. She grinned. That was one perk to city life. Service was really fast.

The ride to Sharp's Design Company was short, since Marty's hotel was nearby, with both in downtown San Francisco. As the cab pulled up in front, she gaped up at the building. The designer in Marty had admired the city's mix of old and new architectural styles which, she had learned on a bus tour she'd taken the day before, was due to a mix of historical events, including the boom in the city in the late 1800s and the earthquake that had caused such devastation in 1906. More modern buildings had cropped up in between, especially as big tech firms moved into the area.

Sharp's Design Company leaned toward the modern side with the whole front of the building made up of windows, but Marty thought that the geometric shapes of glass were probably a nod to the Art Deco style that characterized a lot of other buildings in the area. It was a great look for a design company, current and cutting edge but also not incongruous with the historical areas around it.

Her hands started to sweat as she took the elevator up to the fourteenth floor, where she would meet with Amelia Clapton, her potential boss. Her name had been familiar to Marty, and when she'd looked her up, she'd learned that the woman was responsible for many of Sharp's most iconic designs. On the fourteenth floor, a smiling assistant with an angular haircut greeted Marty with a smile.

"Welcome to Sharp's Design Company," said the woman. She was holding a tablet and wearing a headset. If Marty had tried to walk in heels that high, she worried she would break her neck. "You must be Marty Sims. I'm Kate, Amelia's assistant. The conference room is just through here. Amelia will be with you shortly. Can I get you anything to drink?"

Marty asked for a water and when Kate returned moments later, it wasn't with a glass, as Marty had expected. It was with a very fancy-looking bottle that

Marty was almost too nervous to drink out of. She made herself take a few sips though, to center herself.

Amelia came into the room soon thereafter, and if Kate had seemed stylish to Marty, Amelia looked runway ready. She was wearing a forest green blouse with billowing sleeves that came to a wide cuff at the wrist. The shirt had an elaborate tie at the neck too. She had paired this with wide-legged cream pants that covered all but the pointy toes of her high heeled shoes. Her graying blonde hair was cut into a chic pixie. She looked phenomenal.

"Marty Sims!" exclaimed Amelia, approaching to shake Marty's hand. "Oh my goodness, I'm so glad you came. I have to say, we loved your magazine spread and then I had Kate look you up on social media—young people have the edge on me for those things, although there's some use in these old bones yet, I promise!—and she said your store doesn't have a huge presence but that plenty of past clients have raved about your work. I saw a few pictures and I have to agree, you are the real deal."

Marty took a moment to catch up with all this, which Amelia had said in a rapid-fire pattern while she clasped one of Marty's hands warmly in both of hers. Then Marty smiled, big and effortless. Not only were the things Amelia was saying extremely nice, the woman also had a naturally big energy around her that Marty felt herself get sucked into right away.

"Oh my gosh, Ms. Clapton, that's so nice of you to say!"

"Goodness, call me Amelia." Amelia waved away the formality and sat in the chair next to Marty, instead of across the table, so they turned to look at each other, speaking without a barrier between them. "Now, let's talk all about the position and your designs and what we think we could do to help one another."

Between the woman's warm welcome and the comfort of sinking into a topic she knew extremely well, Marty felt her nerves evaporate. They talked so pleasantly about their current favorite design trends and where they hoped styles would go next that both women were surprised when Kate knocked on the conference room door and let herself in.

"Sorry to interrupt, but Amelia, you have that phone call with Barton's in five minutes and you wanted me to give Marty a tour while you were busy with them."

Amelia looked at her sleek smartwatch in surprise. "Oh, wow, you're right, it's almost time already. I guess time flies when you're having fun." She smiled at Marty. "You're in the best hands ever with Kate. I'll meet you back here after your tour, okay?"

Marty agreed and Amelia hurried out of the room to make her call. When she was gone, Marty looked at Kate. "Is she going to talk to *Barton's* Barton's?"

Kate laughed. "Oh, I know, right?" Barton's Textiles made some of the most luxurious, gorgeous fabrics around—and they cost an arm and a leg. "And it's even crazier than you're thinking—their lead designer is calling Amelia for *advice.*"

"Whoa." Marty couldn't even imagine.

Her shock must have shown on her face, because Kate laughed again, but in a nice way.

"Working here is totally crazy, but in the most amazing way. Come on, I'll show you around and introduce you to everyone."

Kate explained that the design department was on the top four floors of the building. "That's where we'll focus our tour, since that's where you'd be working. The first ten floors are other things, like accounting, human resources, and the magazine." In addition to doing interior design projects, Sharp's put out a quarterly design magazine. Marty always stalked her mailbox when it was due to arrive.

"The first floor has an amazing cafeteria," Kate continued as they walked down a hallway that was chic and comfortable, not at all the kind of bland corporate energy one might expect from such a big company. "We get a discount as employees, which is great, because San Francisco isn't cheap."

"But you like it here?"

"Oh my gosh, I love it," Kate gushed. "And Amelia is seriously the best boss in the world. I have friends at other design companies and they say it can be sort of like an 'old boys' club'—you know, where the people on top want to stay on top without doing any work. Amelia is the complete opposite. She's really invested in mentoring the people who work for her."

Marty was in awe. She imagined what it would be like to work here as Kate took her around, introducing her to different designers, all of whom were nice and welcoming and generously let her take a peek at what they were working on. Except for a few grumbles about how bad traffic could get during rush hour, nobody had a bad word to say about their experience working at Sharp's. For a little while, she let herself fantasize about what it would be like to work here, to come in every morning and whip up beautiful projects with these smart, talented, cool people.

To Marty, the best part of design had always been making people feel at home in their spaces—even if those spaces weren't their actual homes. How many more people would she be able to do that for if she worked at a company like Sharp's, with this kind of reach?

She thought about Darla, who always pushed her to reach for the stars and to not play things so safe. It had been a joking argument between them when Darla had lived in New York City. Marty had always told her sister she would never leave Whale Harbor. But as she looked around Sharp's Design Company, she wondered what she might miss out on by playing things safe. She could hardly believe she was even considering it. Whale Harbor had always been where she planned to spend her life. But this trip had also opened her eyes to new things.

The tour ended, and Kate led her back to her follow-up meeting with Amelia, this time in Amelia's office instead of the conference room. Marty could immediately see that this space was perfect for Amelia, which made sense. It was fashionable and modern, but several shelves of plants made it feel comfortable and welcoming without losing any of the 'cool factor.'

"Oh, Marty, welcome back." Amelia looked up from the sleek laptop on her desk and removed a pair of chunky black glasses. "Did you see everything you wanted to see?"

Marty sat in the plush chair across from the desk. "Everything was amazing! And everyone was so nice too."

"I'm so glad to hear it." Amelia closed her laptop. "Because, Marty, I'd like to officially offer you the position here at Sharp's."

Marty's mouth dropped open. She had thought the interview was going well, but she hadn't expected to be offered the job on the spot! It was tempting to get caught up in the excitement of it all, but Marty knew she had to be smart. She took a deep breath.

"Wow, I'm really honored. I need to take some time to think about it though—moving here would be a big change for me."

Amelia nodded, her smile understanding but a little disappointed. "I get it. I'm afraid I can only give you two days to decide though. We need to fill the position soon."

Marty tried to hide her gulp. Two days was not a lot of time to make such a big decision.

"I understand," she said. "I'll let you know as soon as I decide."

Amelia bid her a friendly farewell and recommended some places that Marty might want to try to eat before she went back to Whale Harbor. Kate sent her a friendly wave as Marty headed to the elevators, and Marty returned the gesture. It wasn't until she was outside in the fresh air that Marty really let herself think about how big and scary this decision was. She was teetering on the edge of something that would change her whole life. On one hand, this would be an amazing professional opportunity for her. But on the other, Whale Harbor was her home... and Wyatt's too. He had seemed so confident when he had said they would work things out, no matter how much distance was between them, but she loved the life they had together in their little town.

As she called another rideshare, the question bounced around and around in her head. Was she really ready to change everything?

CHAPTER EIGHTEEN

Monica was grabbing a new round of surf wax out of the box in her hall closet, since her old round was almost gone, when her phone chimed with a text.

BRADEN: Good morning! I hope it's okay, but I got your address from my mom. I'll swing by and pick you up in about 20 minutes if you're ready to go.

BRADEN: Unless you really were all talk and you're chickening out. *smiley face emoji*

Monica smiled. She liked hearing from him, even if she was going to see him in a few minutes anyway.

MONICA: Not on your life! I'm gonna kick your butt.

MONICA: Oh, and 20 minutes is great.

She slipped her phone back into the pocket of the hoodie she was wearing over her bathing suit, then paused. Braden coming to pick her up made this feel more official... more like a real date. She smoothed her hand over her blonde ponytail, then laughed at herself a little. Like that would matter—her hair was going to get crazy from surfing soon enough.

She tried to put all her focus on packing up her stuff for his arrival, but her nerves got the best of her, and she checked her reflection in the mirror once more. She wore contacts instead of glasses for surfing, so she did look a little different than usual, but definitely not bad. Her bathing suit was flattering—when you went surfing as much as she did, it was worth shelling out for a bathing suit you really liked—and would end up covered by a wetsuit as soon as they got to the beach. It was April, so the days were getting warmer, but the water wouldn't get the memo for another few months.

Eventually Monica decided she was being silly and went back to preparing her stuff. She was probably feeling so nervous because she hadn't been on a real date in such a long time. Not only had she spent the last few years in a relationship, but Connor had been around so rarely that they'd almost never gotten to do the kind of 'date night' stuff that other couples did.

Thinking of Connor made her nerves spike in another direction. Braden wasn't anything like Connor, except for that he wasn't sure that he had a future in Whale Harbor. When she'd made that joke about missing Washington D.C., he'd said he was happy here, but he'd also said he was happy for now. Did that mean he was thinking seriously about going back? D.C. wasn't nearly as far away as San Francisco, and he would definitely come back to visit more often than Connor had, since his mother and soon-to-be stepfather lived here, and he obviously loved them both. At the end of the day though, she knew that she wasn't ready to do another long-distance relationship—she wasn't sure she would ever be ready to go through that again. And she definitely wasn't prepared to risk getting her heart broken again so soon, especially since she had a feeling that a breakup with Braden would be far more painful than the breakup with Connor had been.

You're getting way ahead of yourself, Monica tried to remember. They were just about to go on their first maybe-a-date and she was already worrying about their possible future breakup? It was a morning surfing, not a proposal! She resolved to put her worries aside for now and just enjoy the day.

When Braden pulled up a few minutes later, he came to the door to fetch her, which made it feel even more like a date. He even carried her bags to the car. Unlike some of the first dates she had been on in the past though, it wasn't awkward at all. He gave her the surf report, which he'd looked up before he left home.

"It looks like we're going to have some great waves today," he said as he drove toward the beach. It was the kind of perfect spring morning that made you happy just to be alive and Monica enjoyed the breeze in her hair from the open window. "Great waves for me to ride better than you, that is."

"In your dreams! Don't forget, while you were being a fancy-pants architect in Washington D.C., I was here perfecting my surf style."

He put a hand over his heart like she'd wounded him. "Using my past against me? No fair, Ms. Grey."

She tossed her ponytail playfully as they pulled into the beach cove. "Hey, I play to win. Whatever it takes, Mr. Watson."

As they unloaded their equipment, they set up the terms of their competition, deciding how big a wave had to be for it to count in their game and how long a rider had to stay in the wave in order to earn a point. They shook on it and Monica pushed back the butterflies that she felt when their hands touched. She wasn't about to let something like a crush get in the way of her competitive spirit.

For the next hour, they caught wave after wave. She had to admit, Braden was a really good surfer, but that only made her more determined to be better. She focused on that instead of noticing how handsome and strong he looked in his formfitting wetsuit.

When the chill of the water was starting to get uncomfortable even through their wetsuits, they agreed on five more minutes to end the competition, each marking the time on their waterproof watches. He glided along his last wave in a picture-perfect ride just as the agreed-upon time hit. After he finished, Braden paddled out toward where Monica was floating, seated on her board.

"You played a good game, Grey, but that's a tiebreaker to me." He pretended to show off his muscles and she splashed some water in his direction.

"No way. Time hit before you were done. It doesn't count."

"It totally counts," he insisted. "It's like in basketball—if you start the shot before the buzzer sounds, it still counts if it goes in the basket."

She shook her head, affecting sadness. "I don't know how to tell you this, but there are no balls in surfing, Braden. Just surfboards."

"Oh, you're *so* funny."

He reached over like he was about to push her off her surfboard, so she grabbed his board too. If she was going swimming, so was he. The motion brought their boards side by side. They looked at each other for a second and then both leaned in for a sweet, soft kiss. Monica was getting a bit lost in the moment until a rogue wave jostled their boards, not enough to knock them into the water, but enough to cause them to separate.

"Oh, gosh," she said.

For a minute they floated, not quite looking at one another. Then Braden broke the silence.

"Geez, I'm sorry, Mon." He rubbed the back of his neck, expression rueful. "I probably shouldn't have done that. I know you just broke up with your boyfriend."

She shook her head. "It's okay. Things between me and Connor were over long before they were really over, if you get what I mean. So, in some ways, the breakup doesn't feel as fresh as it would otherwise. I think the main thing that makes me feel hesitant is that you don't know yet if you're staying in Whale Harbor, and one thing my relationship with Connor taught me is that I don't think I'm cut out for long distance."

He nodded. "That makes sense. I wanted to have an answer for you before I made any kind of move but... I got caught up in the moment."

Monica blushed, feeling pleased that he had been making plans to make a move, even if they weren't set in stone.

"I definitely got caught up too."

"But, Mon?" He caught her eye. "I want to make sure that you know that even if I don't know where I'll be living long term, I do know one thing. I think you're really special. And I really like you."

She bit her lip as her heart started to race. She wasn't sure how to respond and so she was grateful when a bigger wave swept past, nearly knocking them from their boards.

"I think maybe that's a hint that it's time to go in," she said, laughing from the jostling motion.

"I'm getting kind of cold, anyway. Let's go in."

They paddled to shore, Monica deep in thought. She looked at Braden, paddling ahead of her, his long arms propelling him quickly through the water. He really was so handsome, she thought, feeling her heart begin to race again. And as good as it felt to hear that he really liked her, it made her nervous too. She worried that coming out here this morning had been a mistake, as fun as it had been, because she was starting to really fall for him, and he might be getting ready to leave Whale Harbor for good.

Darla waited on the sidewalk outside the art museum, her insides fluttering with excitement. Rick had texted her to say he would be there in fifteen minutes—she checked her phone—twelve minutes ago. She hoped he would hurry... while still driving safely, of course.

When she saw his car pull into the little lot next to the museum, she waved eagerly. She couldn't wait to show him all the final details now that they were in place. This had been the project into which Darla had poured her heart and soul these last few months and she had just finished everything this morning. That had been exciting enough, to see the finished product for herself, but there was something about showing everything to her fiancé that made it seem even more real. She hoped he loved it, especially after business at the museum had caused them to delay their wedding planning so many times.

"Hey, honey!" Rick called as he approached, jogging a little to get there faster. Darla's heart swelled. She still felt eager to see him every day too. She hoped she always felt that way. "Guess what? We had the most amazing whale sighting this morning. The big guy couldn't have been more than a hundred feet from the boat. The tourists went nuts —and I can't blame them."

He reached out to her as he spoke, giving her a quick peck hello.

"That's amazing," she replied. "You know, I don't miss the days where you would write to me about your days in a letter. I much prefer hearing it in person."

He gave her a teasing look. "How would you know? I never sent any of those letters."

"You know I read them after I got back!"

He slung an arm around her shoulders. "I know, I know." He shook his head sadly, but there was a smile playing about his lips. "You just always have to remind a man of the low point in his life, huh?"

Darla swatted playfully at his stomach, but he caught her hand and kissed it, instead.

"All right, you got me. You know I love it too. Now, are you going to show me this museum or what?"

"Wait, don't look yet! You have to get the full effect."

She reached up to cover Rick's eyes, fumbling for the door as she tried to open it and be a makeshift blindfold at the same time. Since he was taller than her, their steps inside were stumbling, and they both laughed. When they got far enough into the building that the door could swing closed behind them, she removed her hands.

"Ta da!"

He looked around the small space and, as he did, Darla tried to see the museum through his eyes. She'd been working so closely on the project for such a long time that it was hard to picture what it would look like to someone who hadn't been consumed by the nitty-gritty details. He turned in a full circle, a small smile spreading across his face, becoming bigger with every new thing he saw.

"What do you think?" she asked, a little bit nervously. His approval was probably the most important to her out of everyone she knew. Not only was he the love of her life, but he was an artist too.

"Oh, sweetheart." His voice was low and

impressed. "You did *such* an amazing job. It's incredible in here! You should be so proud of yourself."

She jumped into his outstretched arms. "I'm so glad you like it!"

"Were you worried?" His tone was teasing but she thought maybe he meant the question too.

"Not really... More excited, I guess. But I really wanted you to love it."

Rick gave her another quick kiss. "I'm pretty sure I'd love anything you did, but this is objectively amazing. Walk me through everything—I want the insider's tour."

She pointed out the different areas, which were separated by temporary walls that could be moved to open the space up or cordoned off to make smaller nooks for more intimate viewings.

"Those are really nice," he said, nodding his head. "I've seen some that look kind of shabby, but these aren't like that at all."

"Right? Marty helped me find those—you know she has the inside scoop on all things design. Anyway, over there is the kids' area. It's more interactive so that they're not just looking at art, they're learning to become little artists themselves."

"Oh, they'll have so much fun with that." He

wrapped an arm around her waist. "It's brilliant, because the kids will want to stay longer and the parents will have more time to check out everything without little hands tugging them to go."

Darla smiled up at him. "That section was inspired by you, actually—I never would have been here to do this if you hadn't asked me to come teach that art class last summer. Teaching there made me realize how important it is to me to foster a love of arts in future generations as well as create it for myself."

He looked genuinely touched. "I'm honored."

She gave him a tight squeeze. "You changed my whole life," she said quietly. "This whole beautiful, wonderful life—I wouldn't have it without you."

He squeezed back just as lovingly. "That means so much to me, honey, but don't sell yourself short. *You* made this place a reality and I am so proud of you I want to run out into the street and tell everyone I see that they have to come in and check it out right this second."

Darla laughed. "We aren't open yet."

"I didn't say I'm *going to* do it, just that I wanted to." He rested his cheek on the top of her head. "Seriously though, I'm so happy for you. You've really put yourself on the map in this town, and we're all better off for it. This is a really special space, and the whole town is going to appreciate it."

He paused, and when he spoke again, his voice held a tiny bit of smugness.

"And I'm really excited because *I* got to see it first."

CHAPTER NINETEEN

Wyatt picked up his phone, then put it down with a sigh. He should get started making dinner, anyway. Just because his girlfriend was gone didn't mean he had to go 'full bachelor' and eat a frozen pizza or something. There was some chicken in the fridge. Maybe he should go out and put it on the grill, since the weather was nice...

Less than five minutes later he was picking the phone up again and calling Marty. It was the third time today that he'd tried to get a hold of her. The phone rang and rang and eventually her voice mail picked up.

Hi, you've reached Marty Sims! Please leave a message and—

He hung up, not bothering to leave a message.

Bad enough that he kept calling over and over, he didn't need to leave a bunch of voice mails on top of that. What would he say, anyway?

Hey, Mar, I know you told me yesterday that you had a great interview and hadn't made a choice yet, but I'm getting pretty nervous over here so if you're going to accept, do you think you could just rip off the band-aid?

That was the real problem, he thought—he was getting the sinking feeling that Marty wanted to accept the position. He wondered if this was how Marty had felt, back when it wasn't certain they'd get together. When he'd returned to Whale Harbor after his divorce, she hadn't been convinced at first that he'd outgrown the wishy-washy ways of his younger self. That was what had led to his divorce, after all. She hadn't known whether to believe he could ever really settle down, could ever really be happy with the quiet life that Whale Harbor promised.

He was though. He was happier than he could ever remember being, actually.

That's all due to Marty, he thought, trying not to let his fingers twitch toward his phone again. At the end of the day, she was everything to him. And if that meant that it was his turn to be the steady one for a while as she went off and had her big adventure, went and chased her dreams... He could do that. Being with her had taught him a lot about himself, and one thing he had learned was that he was capable of being a reliable man. He found he actually liked living that kind of settled-in life. But he understood a hunger for adventure too, and Marty had lived in Whale Harbor her whole life. Maybe this was her time for adventuring.

Wyatt knew he would support her no matter what. But that still didn't mean he wasn't really nervous to hear her decision.

He was so lost in thought that when his phone rang, he jumped, startling Bertram, who had been lounging near his feet.

"Sorry, Bert!" he called after the offended tail that was disappearing around the corner, even as he lunged for his phone.

Wyatt used to be the kind of guy who could play it cool when a woman called him, but being with Marty had turned him to mush. He didn't mind it one bit. The phone had barely started its second ring when he put it to his ear.

"Hey, honey!"

The background of the call was noisy with the hustle and bustle of the city. Even over the phone it sounded lively and exciting.

"Wyatt, hi! Sorry, I missed your calls before. I was exploring." Marty sounded breathless and happy.

He felt a subtle sinking in his stomach, but reminded himself not to get worried before he had something to worry about. "Oh yeah? Did you see anything good?"

"Oh my gosh, so much! I went down to the pier today—it's crazy how different the Pacific looks from the Atlantic! Then I had the most amazing lunch at this restaurant that Amelia suggested. The seafood here is definitely a different style than Whale Harbor, but it's amazing. I had these delicious oysters while I sat looking out over the bay, and an asparagus salad, and the most incredible French bread I think I've ever had in my whole life."

"Wow, that sounds fantastic." He felt a pang of sadness that he wasn't there to enjoy this with her, and hoped this wasn't what their lives would look like from now on.

She laughed, a big, joyful sound, on the other end of the line. "It really was. I mean, it was a *lot* fancier than I'm used to and definitely more of a one-time treat than a regular thing, but I had so much fun. I just bought this apple fritter that everyone said I should try, but I thought I should walk back to my hotel before digging in, try to work up an appetite. It looked so good, I couldn't resist though."

The background noise got suddenly quieter, and Wyatt assumed she had gone inside, maybe into her hotel. He wished he could picture her surroundings. Maybe it would help her feel less far away.

"Honey," he said gently, hating to bring down her cheerful mood. "Have you made a decision about the job yet? It sounds like you're really liking it out there."

There was a pause, and his stomach sank further.

"I haven't decided yet. I am really loving the city, but..." Marty paused and he desperately wanted to probe further, ask what she was thinking. "I just haven't decided. Can you wait one more day?"

"Of course, Mar." Still, he couldn't hold back the tiny sigh that escaped him. "I'd do anything for you, you know that."

"I'm really sorry." Her voice sounded small. "I know it's hard."

"Hey, now," he protested, hating how this conversation had dulled her sparkling attitude over her day. "Don't apologize. It is hard, I won't lie, but I would have to be a real jerk to push you to make a decision this big faster just for my sake."

"Hey, watch it. That's my boyfriend you're

calling a jerk. Don't make me fight you," she teased.

He smiled, happy she sounded bright again. "Oh, man, I would never dare fight you. You're too tough for me, Sims!" She laughed.

They talked for a few more minutes, but Wyatt still needed to make dinner and Marty sounded tired from her big day, so they hung up, promising to speak the next day and saying they loved one another. He slid his phone into his pocket and bent down to scratch Peaches, who had begun winding in between his legs as he talked. Peaches always knew when one of 'her people' was upset.

"Guess you heard me talking to your mom, huh?" he asked the orange cat.

Peaches meowed, but rubbed her head against his hand as if to say, *I'm listening, but only so long as you keep these pets coming.*

"The thing is," he continued, because sometimes saying things out loud helped you to work through them, "I just love her so much. But it's not just that. I love our whole life here. I love you rascals too, even when Trouble thinks it's a fun game to knock my toothbrush off the counter." He shook his head, thinking about the cat's antics. He couldn't imagine his life without them anymore. "I'm kind of scared, I guess. Change is always scary, and I'm not in charge of this one. But I would never forgive myself if I made your mom feel pressured to give up on something she really wanted just to make me happy."

Peaches headbutted him and looked at him with eyes that Wyatt could have sworn were judgmental.

"You're right, you're right. I just need to be patient and see what she says tomorrow. Thanks, Peaches. You always know what to say."

Peaches headbutted him again, this time a bit more softly. Wyatt chuckled. Sometimes it really did seem like the cats understood things.

Bertram came around the corner then, apparently having forgiven Wyatt for startling him. He waited patiently at Wyatt's feet.

"You too, Bert," he said. "You're also the best."

As if on cue, Macy and Trouble came racing into the room like two little cannonballs, skidding to a stop to join their brother and sister.

Despite his worries, Wyatt laughed aloud at the sight of the four little faces, all peering up at him curiously.

"I didn't forget the two of you, don't worry. Now, what do we say we all have some dinner?"

The cats enthusiastically—and very loudly—decided they all agreed with that idea.

CHAPTER TWENTY

When Monica spotted Braden's car outside the B&B as she drove past on the day after their surfing date, on her way to the grocery store to pick up some odds and ends for dinner, she almost didn't stop. It wasn't that she didn't want to see Braden. It was the opposite, actually. Her heart actually gave a little leap when she saw his car. That little leap made her concerned about how deep her feelings for him were growing.

Just before she went around the corner that would take her to Whale Harbor's little downtown area, however, she let out a small sigh and headed toward the back area of the property, where she could park. She was being silly. Even if she wasn't yet sure if she wanted to pursue a relationship with

Braden, given his uncertain future in Whale Harbor, she knew she wanted to keep up with being his friend. Avoiding him was not friendly behavior. She parked and headed inside.

"Hello?" she called, not wanting to repeat the events of the other night, when each had suspected the other of being an intruder.

He poked his head out from the area that would become the downstairs bathroom, a smile breaking across his face when he saw her. "Hey!"

When they approached each other in the hallway, she felt a little awkward. Should she hug him? She wanted to, but wasn't sure it would be a good idea, given how uncertain everything was between them. They stopped with a few feet still separating them, and there was an uncomfortable moment where they couldn't quite make eye contact.

Then Braden broke the silence. "I hope I didn't come on too strong yesterday, Mon. I meant what I said. I think you're incredible. But I don't want to make you feel uncomfortable or lose our friendship."

"You didn't!" She hastened to reassure him, then paused. "Can we go sit in the front room? I guess we should probably talk about everything."

He nodded, and they headed into the bright room, warmly lit by morning sunlight. There wasn't any furniture yet, but they perched in the window seat, which would make a perfect place for curling up with a book once she got a cushion to make the hard wood a bit more comfortable.

"I think I owe you an explanation," she began.

He shook his head, frowning. "You don't owe me anything."

"Okay, okay." She tried again. "I *want* to explain things. I want to lay all my cards out on the table."

"Okay, that's different, then."

He leaned back against the wood that bordered the window, his posture relaxed. Still, she thought maybe he looked a little nervous. Oddly enough, that comforted her. She was glad she wasn't the only one feeling butterflies over their relationship... or whatever it was between them.

She took a deep breath. "First off, I want to say that I think you're great too. All night last night I was wishing I had been clearer about that."

Braden smiled. "I get it, I promise."

She gave him a small smile. He really was so wonderful and understanding.

"I know you do. And I wish..." She cleared her throat. "I wish I wasn't bringing any past baggage into things between you and me. I promise that I know you're completely different from Connor. It's just hard for me to look at any relationship without considering the lens of where I've been, you know?"

He nodded at her. "That makes complete sense. I don't think looking out for what you want—and need—from a relationship is 'baggage,' though. I think it's a smart move, actually."

Monica appreciated this, but she still wanted to make sure he really understood her. She thought for a moment about how to phrase things.

"When I was with Connor," she began, "I spent a long time thinking that if I just waited, if I was just patient and practical instead of letting my hurt feelings dictate my actions, that things would work out in the end. And that meant telling myself not to worry about things that I was really worried about."

She took a deep breath. In some ways, the hardest part of her breakup wasn't losing Connor, since things had already been so tense between them for so long. It was more painful, in a lot of ways, to realize how wrong she'd been for so long, and how easily she'd allowed Connor to treat her shabbily.

Braden waited patiently while she gathered her thoughts.

"I guess," she continued after a long moment, "that I'm learning to trust my feelings again. But that's tricky too, because my feelings are telling me that getting into another long-distance relationship would be a mistake... but they're also telling me that you're a great guy and worth some risk." She said this last part with her eyes on her lap, not wanting to meet his gaze as she made her confession.

He shifted in the window seat until they were seated next to one another and wrapped an arm around her shoulders. She let herself sink into his warm embrace, imagining, just for a moment, what it might feel like if their worries were behind them and they could begin to grow closer as a romantic couple. It was a really nice image and she had to suppress a little sigh.

"Thanks for being so honest with me," he said, pressing his cheek against the top of her head where it rested against his shoulder. "I already knew you were special, but now I know you're brave too."

Part of Monica wanted to brush this off as a joke, but instead she let the warmth of his compliment sink in. This was another way Braden was different from Connor. Connor had always given her token compliments that felt generic, whereas Braden said things that made her feel like he really appreciated who she was, deep down. She not only liked him, she liked how he made her feel about herself too.

He shifted his position so they were looking at

one another. She was sorry to lose the comfort of his hug, but knew some conversations were best face-to-face.

"I want to be transparent with you too," he said, reaching out to gently hold one of her hands. "I don't know what the future holds." This made her stomach clench nervously, but he continued. "For a while, I was just waiting to see how things went, taking the decision to stay in Whale Harbor or go back to Washington day by day. But getting to know you... Well, it's making me think more about the future. I know you got hurt before, and I'm definitely not interested in being the reason you get hurt again, so I don't want to give you a definite answer until I'm totally, completely sure, but..." He paused and gave her that sweet smile of his. She knew she was blushing. "More and more every day, I can picture us building a future here."

"Yeah?" Her voice was breathless.

He reached up his free hand to touch her cheek lightly. "Yeah. I promise I'm not going to keep you waiting forever. I'll have an answer for you soon."

She nodded. Although waiting to know what Braden planned was difficult, Monica appreciated his commitment to making sure his decision was final before he said anything that would make her hope for their future together.

"That means a lot to me," she said.

His smile got bigger, breaking some of the tension, which was heavy but not unpleasant. "One thing I can promise though." He waved an arm around the room. "I'll be here long enough to make your vision come to life."

He looked so excited on her behalf that her heart swelled with affection. The feeling was so strong that it made her brave, and she leaned forward to give Braden a long, lingering kiss.

When they pulled apart, he was smiling. "Wow, if I knew helping you do construction would get me kissed, I would have started taking a hammer everywhere I went weeks ago," he teased.

She grinned and swatted at his shoulder playfully. "Okay, then, funny man, let's get to work."

And they happily spent a few hours working side by side, Monica's heart feeling like it was glowing in her chest.

After a pleasant afternoon working at the B&B, enjoying knowing Monica was there with him even if she spent most of her time in a different room than him, Braden stopped by the bakery and got a box of donuts before stopping by Thomas's apartment. His soon-to-be stepfather was living in his old apartment until he and Gabrielle got married, which Braden thought was very sweet. The two of them often giggled like teenagers in love when they planned their wedding and marriage, and it made Braden feel a lot lighter to see his mother happy again after losing his father.

Thomas answered the door right away when Braden knocked. "What a wonderful surprise!" he said, opening the door wide. "Come on in, son. *And* you brought donuts? I'm a lucky man, indeed."

Braden didn't even try to hide his smile. Thomas was a great guy, and he was happy for his own sake as well as for his mother's that he was in their lives now. And he liked that he and Thomas were building their own relationship too. Thomas treated him like a son without treating him like a little kid, which was a great balance, Braden thought—though he didn't have much experience with how things went when your parents were dating. Even if his relationship with his father had been complicated, he knew he was lucky that his parents had stayed married. Divorce could be hard for kids.

Thomas's apartment was small and neat, with bookshelves that were absolutely crammed with reading material of all kinds. *Monica would love it here,* Braden thought with a private smile. Thomas's laptop was open on his kitchen table, but as they walked into the kitchen, he closed it immediately and put it away.

"To what do I owe this pleasure?" Thomas asked. "Can I pour you a cup of coffee to go with those donuts? It's decaf."

"Oh, yeah, that would be great." Coffee and donuts were a perfect combination. "And I was hoping to pick your brain about something."

Thomas returned to the table with two mugs and a carton of milk tucked under his arm. "Oh, I see. So these are ulterior motive donuts," he teased.

Braden laughed, taking one of the mugs and adding a dollop of milk, before handing it back to Thomas to do the same. He took two donuts out of the box—a chocolate glazed for him and an apple fritter for Thomas.

"Maybe more of a bribe than an ulterior motive, since it's nothing bad. I just need a bit of advice."

"About Monica Grey?" Thomas punctuated the question with a hearty bite of apple fritter.

Braden looked at him in surprise. "How did you

know?" Then he laughed to himself as he realized the answer to his own question. "Whale Harbor gossip mill." He shook his head affectionately.

Thomas smiled and took a sip of coffee to wash down his mouthful of pastry. "Your mom keeps me in the loop on everything. Although I have to say, I was a little surprised to hear the rumors."

Braden frowned. "You were?"

"Not because you don't make a nice couple, son. She's a great girl and you know I think the world of you." Thomas cupped both hands around his mug contemplatively. "I was just a little surprised that you were thinking of starting something up here if you're still thinking about going to Washington."

Braden sighed. "That's exactly what I need advice about, actually. I've always liked Monica, but my feelings are starting to get more serious. But I haven't decided for sure yet if I'm staying, and her last relationship ended because of distance." *And because that Connor guy was a huge jerk*, he thought to himself. He didn't say that part out loud though. He wasn't sure if Monica would appreciate him spreading Connor's infidelity around, even to someone like Thomas, who was completely trustworthy.

Thomas nodded. "And you're asking because I

made my move to Whale Harbor permanent for your mother?"

"Yeah. Plus, you started dating Mom after she lost somebody. I know a breakup isn't the same as the death of a husband, but..."

"But there's hurt there in both situations," Thomas finished for him, still nodding. "That's a smart way to think about it. And it sounds like you're already doing the most important part—being conscious of the pain that she has in her past, and doing what you can to avoid adding to that pain."

"I really don't want to hurt her," Braden confirmed.

Thomas took another bite of his apple fritter before responding. "Well, I think my best advice here is to make sure you're gentle, patient, and honest. You don't want to hurt her, but you don't want to hurt yourself either, and deciding where you're going to live for the rest of your life is a big decision. When I was deciding to stay in Whale Harbor, I pictured my life here, with your mom, or in Boston, without her. I tried to be as fair as possible, looking at the good and bad of both options. Obviously, staying here was the right choice for me but—" Thomas shot Braden a sly grin and lowered his voice, even though there was nobody else there to hear them. "—don't tell your Ms. Grey this, but I do sometimes miss that big library we had in Boston."

Both men laughed for a moment.

"You mean, you don't have every book ever written right here in this apartment?" Braden teased, waving an arm around at the crowded bookshelves.

"I might be missing one or two. Anyway, it sounds like Monica has told you what she wants. Now you just have to decide what you want and communicate that to her."

Braden nodded thoughtfully. He had been thinking a lot of the same things, but it still helped to hear Thomas say them out loud.

"Thanks," he said after a pause to process his thoughts. "I don't have the answer yet, but I think I'm getting there."

Thomas stood to clear the dishes, first clapping a friendly hand on Braden's shoulder. "Well, I don't want to tip the scales, but I certainly wouldn't mind you sticking around. Especially," he added with a glimmer in his eye, "if you keep bringing these donuts when you show up."

Braden helped Thomas clean up, chatted for a few more minutes, and then bid the older man goodnight. As he drove home, he thought about everything they had talked about. He knew he could be patient with Monica—she was worth it. And they were both doing a good job being honest with one another.

So there was really only one question left: would he be happy remaining in Whale Harbor to be with her?

CHAPTER TWENTY-ONE

"Now boarding Flight 2741, direct service to Providence, Rhode Island."

The voice rang out over the intercom, jolting Marty out of her sleepy haze. It was barely six o'clock in the morning, and she had already been up for hours. She had originally been scheduled on a flight out that afternoon, but last night, as she had been eating yet another delicious dinner and thinking about the answer to Sharp's that was due this morning, a sudden bolt of clarity had hit her.

Yes, the position at Sharp's Design Company was a great opportunity. It would let her do bigger and more elaborate designs than she'd otherwise have the opportunity to do.

But the idea of doing all that exciting work, she

realized, meant nothing to her if she didn't have Wyatt by her side.

As soon as she'd realized that, everything else had fallen into place. She had faith they could work it out if she moved to California, but the more she thought about doing the long-distance thing, or having him move with her to start over, the less appealing it sounded. She'd be able to do bigger things at Sharp's, but bigger wasn't always better. She liked her little store in Whale Harbor, liked that she knew most of her customers by name and had known many of them for years. And she loved the life she was building with Wyatt. She loved their morning routines, and the way she knew that Bertram would be snuggled next to Wyatt's legs every day when their alarms went off. She loved that they always had a quick kiss goodbye on the same street corner before they went to their respective stores. She didn't want to change all that.

Once the decision had been made, Marty had found herself eager to get back to her regular life as soon as possible. She'd quickly paid her check for dinner, made one last important stop, and then gone back to her hotel to reschedule her flight so she was on the first plane out this morning.

The first plane, it turned out, left *very* early, and

while the part of her that was eager to return to Wyatt was excited about that, it had been really hard to drag herself out of her comfy bed while it was still dark out.

With the help of a large cup of coffee, she woke up just as the boarding process was starting, and as the plane took off, every minute bringing her closer to home, she was filled with a restless energy that made the flight seem like it lasted forever. She was too excited to even pay attention to the in-flight movie, although she tried, just to pass the time. Most of her attention, however, was fixated on the object she fiddled between her hands as she counted the minutes until she got home.

When her flight landed, she hurried off the plane, then had to bounce impatiently on her toes while she waited for her suitcase to arrive at the baggage claim. She got a rideshare back to Whale Harbor. She hadn't told anyone she was coming home early, because she wanted to surprise Wyatt. Whale Harbor was amazing for so many things, but keeping a secret was not one of them.

She went directly to Wyatt's Quads, not even caring that her hair was no doubt frizzy and mussed from the long journey. She hurried inside.

"Oh, hey, Marty!" said Devin, one of the

workers. He was a college kid who had recently started working with Wyatt, and always had a smile for everyone. "Looking for Wyatt?"

"Yeah, is he here?"

Devin shook his head. "Sorry, no. He went out to the dunes. Do you want me to call him?" He gestured with the store's phone.

"No, that's okay." Marty wanted to see him herself. "Can I borrow one of the quads though? Wyatt taught me how to drive them. I want to go out and meet him."

"Of course!" Devin handed her a set of keys from one of the rental quads. She thanked him and headed out.

The ride to the dunes was short, the bouncy drive a perfect fit for her emotional state. She felt bouncy inside too. When she got to the dunes, she saw Wyatt right away. He was driving up and down, more idly than with the kind of high-speed energy he usually preferred. At the top of a dune, she got off her quad, and removed her helmet, waving both arms to get his attention.

He saw her immediately, his quad picking up speed as it headed in her direction. When he reached her, he shut off the engine and hopped off, carelessly tossing his helmet aside and revealing the enormous grin on his face.

"Oh my gosh," he said, scooping her up in a huge hug. "What are you doing here? You're not supposed to be back until tonight!" He spun her around in a circle and gave her a warm, welcoming kiss.

As they kissed, Marty felt the rightness of her decision sink in even further. He tasted like home.

When they pulled apart, she looked up at him, her grin mirroring his. "I couldn't wait. I had to see you and tell you my decision. I turned down the job."

She saw the hope flash in his eye but because he was the best boyfriend ever as far as she was concerned, he still paused to peer at her. "You're sure?" he asked. "I don't want you to feel like you have to give up something big for me."

She shook her head. "I'm not giving up anything. The city was awesome and the company was amazing, but it's not my forever place. *This* is where I want to be permanently. Here, in Whale Harbor. With you."

His grin was blinding. "That's what I want too, honey. You and me."

"Well..." She gently disentangled herself from his arms and reached into her pocket to pull out the item she'd been fiddling with all the way back from

California, the important stop she'd made the night before, once everything had fallen mentally into place.

Wyatt gaped at her as she dropped to one knee, right there in the sand. "Wyatt Jameson," she asked, feeling tears of happiness already begin to gather in her eyes. "Will you marry me?"

He reached down and scooped her back up into his arms, kissing her passionately. Marty threw her arms around his neck, then pulled back.

"Wait a minute, is that a yes?"

"Of course it's a yes," he said, kissing her again. "You won't believe this, but I actually have a ring for you at home."

"No way!"

He laughed. "I'm not kidding! I was going to wait until after you decided about the job, because I didn't want you to feel pressured, but I was going to ask either way. We have a reservation at The Blue Crab tomorrow. I was going to tell you it was a 'welcome home' dinner when secretly it was a proposal dinner."

"Well, now it can be a 'we're engaged!' dinner," she said, sliding the ring onto his finger.

It was a simple gold ring with a line of sandstone in the middle, as a nod to Wyatt's love of riding his quad on the beach—which made it perfect that this was where she'd popped the question. She knew it wasn't strictly traditional for men to have an engagement ring, but she hadn't wanted to propose empty-handed, and when she'd seen this ring, she'd known it was 'the one.'

They kissed for a little while longer, although they kept having to break apart to laugh with happiness and give each other goofy, loving looks. When the sun started to set—sooner than Marty's body expected, since she was still on California time—Wyatt turned them back toward their quads.

"Come on," she said. "Let's go home, then it's your turn to propose to me."

He revved his engine. "Oh yeah? You gonna say yes?"

She gave him a playful shrug. "Guess you're going to have to wait and see."

He laughed. "Being married to you is always gonna be an adventure, huh?"

She winked. "You bet it is." They rode off, their laughter snatched away by the wind.

CHAPTER TWENTY-TWO

While Marty waited for Monica to arrive for their lunch date at the Clownfish Eatery, she couldn't stop admiring her engagement ring from Wyatt. It wasn't a traditional ring. Instead, Wyatt had chosen an oval-shaped aquamarine surrounded by a halo of diamonds. The diamonds weren't in a perfect circle; tiny sets of three stones protruded out from the central aquamarine almost like leaves or petals. The whole thing was set in a narrow gold band. It was the perfect ring for a designer like her, elegant and beautiful, of course, but also different enough that it would always stand out.

Marty was so caught up in sighing over the piece of jewelry—and what it represented—that she didn't notice Monica's approach until her friend was right in front of her.

"Oh my goodness!" exclaimed Monica, snatching Marty's hand to peer at the ring. "Is this what I think it is?"

Marty knew she'd never be able to hide her infectious grin, so she didn't even bother trying. "Shoot! I was going to hide my hands under the table and then tell you the whole story, whipping the ring out as the big reveal at the end!"

Monica rolled her eyes affectionately, chuckling at her friend's antics. "Okay, well I still want to hear the whole story though—*obviously*."

Marty told her everything, starting with her big realization in California, then moving on to her early-morning flight home, meeting Wyatt out on the dunes, and their mutual proposals. When she was done, Monica was looking at her with stars in her eyes.

"That's *so* romantic. I mean, your story was already so romantic." Monica, a book lover to her core, waved her arm like she could see the tale laid out before her. "Best friends for years, separated by circumstance, then finding each other again and falling in love? It's perfect. Only now you're getting married, so it's the whole fairy tale package."

Marty giggled over Monica's dramatic presentation of her relationship with Wyatt. "Don't those fairy tales usually end with something horrible and gory?"

"You're right. Your story is even *better* than a fairy tale."

Monica gushed over Marty's ring for a few minutes longer, only stopping to order their food. When their orders arrived—crab cakes for Marty and a bowl of clam chowder and a hunk of crusty, fresh bread for Monica—they dug in with gusto, their conversation shifting to Monica's plans for the B&B.

"So, now that I'm officially staying in Whale Harbor for the long term—" Monica gave a supportive squeak of excitement. "—when can I come over to start planning designs with you?" Marty asked.

Monica took a sip of her water before answering. "Soon, I think. Braden is almost done with the inside renovations and will be moving out to the porch, probably in the next few days. I'll let you know as soon as I know more—I'm talking to him right after we're done here, so I'll text you about what he says."

Marty looked her friend up and down. Monica looked lit up with excitement—but was that just about her new business venture or was it about the contractor who was helping make her dreams a reality? She decided to tread carefully. She thought Monica and Braden would be perfect together, but her friend was still coming off a painful breakup. She didn't want to apply more pressure than she should.

"It sounds like Braden is planning to be in Whale Harbor for a while, then," she said offhandedly, although she was watching Monica's reaction closely.

Monica sighed and fiddled with the crust of bread still left on her plate. "He hasn't said he's decided for sure, and he promised he would tell me as soon as he had made up his mind, so I think that means things are still uncertain." Marty made an inquisitive noise and Monica looked up at her. "We may have had some… moments recently," Monica admitted.

Marty propped her chin on her hand. "Moments?"

She listened attentively as Monica told her about a surf date that ended in a kiss, how she pulled back, still feeling uncertain, and then how she and Braden had talked things out… and kissed a little more.

"I'm just not sure how to move forward," Monica confessed. "We both have feelings for one another, but until his decision about staying in Whale Harbor is final, I feel stuck. Part of me wants to throw caution to the wind and just go for it, but another part of me is scared to, after what happened with Connor."

Marty reached out and squeezed Monica's hand. "I know you know this, but it's worth saying: Braden isn't Connor. And taking a chance is scary, but..." She drew out the last word as she wiggled her finger, the light glinting off her ring. Taking a chance on love was the best thing she had ever done. "Look where it got Wyatt and me."

After a long Friday spent at the docks, going through some essential but boring paperwork for his business, Braden sent a text to his mother.

BRADEN: Long day spent hunched over papers—could use some face time with the best mom ever. Want to have dinner? I could pick up some takeout.

BRADEN: Face time with the best mom ever *and* her fiancé, of course. *smiley face emoji*

To his surprise, his mother didn't text back. Instead, his phone rang in his hand.

"Hey, Mom!"

"Braden, sweetie! Normally I would say we would love to have dinner, but we can't tonight."

He juggled his phone against his ear while he fished around in his pocket for his car keys. "Oh, no? Did you guys already eat?"

"Well, we did, actually, but..." His mother's voice trailed off and he heard her whispering to someone, presumably Thomas, in the background. "Can I tell him?" she was saying. This caused him to blink in confusion. He didn't worry though, because her voice sounded just as cheerful as usual, maybe even more so.

"Mom? Is everything okay?"

His mother's laughter grew louder as she put the phone back to her ear. "Yes, honey, everything is wonderful. The real reason Thomas and I can't join you for dinner is that we're out of town. And not only that—we eloped!"

"*What?*" In his excitement and surprise, Braden dropped his phone. He quickly scooped it back up, glad it wasn't broken. "You eloped?"

"Yes! We talked about it and since we had both done the big wedding thing the first time around, we wanted to stay small. And then we talked about it some more and decided what we really wanted was to be married as soon as possible. So we packed our bags, hurried to the airport, and went." Gabrielle's voice got a little hesitant. "You aren't mad we did it without you, are you?"

"Oh my gosh, Mom, no!' Braden exclaimed. "I'm so happy for you guys!" He ran a hand through his hair. Good for them, going after what made them happy. Then he realized what he'd forgotten. "You surprised me so much I almost forgot: congratulations!"

"Thank you," Gabrielle said. "I have to say, it feels good to be a married woman again. I feel like I couldn't possibly deserve to be this happy."

"Don't be silly, Mom. If anyone deserves it, it's definitely you. And that new stepdad of mine, of course. Tell him congrats from me too, okay? Now, you don't want to spend your special day on the phone—enjoy your trip and tell me all about it when you get back."

His mother sounded like a giddy schoolgirl as she bid him goodbye, and after he hung up, he found himself smiling dopily over how happy he was for her. One of the best parts of coming back to Whale Harbor had been getting to see his mother fall in love, as well as getting to build up their relationship again. He had missed her a lot when he'd lived in Washington D.C., and wished now that he hadn't let his difficult relationship with his father make him grow somewhat distant from his mother too.

That line of thinking took him to the other best part about moving back to Whale Harbor: getting closer to Monica. Even though it had been simple, spending time with her at the B&B had been amazing. It was easy to picture himself working side by side with her there in a more long-term kind of way. Just because he could picture something didn't mean it would make him happy though, he reminded himself. But he *felt* happy when he was with her. He even felt happy just thinking about her.

He daydreamed about Monica as he drove into Whale Harbor, imagining what she would do if he tugged her cute blonde ponytail like he was a kid on a playground with a crush. Last time he'd been working with her at the B&B he'd been so tempted to do that, and he could just imagine her outraged expression that wouldn't do much to hide how hard she had to try not to laugh.

Since he wasn't having dinner with his mother after all, he decided just to stop by the Harvest Grocery Store and buy some of the ready-made food they had at the deli counter. After his long day, he didn't feel like cooking for just himself, and a ham sandwich with some potato salad sounded like the perfect, easy dinner. He pulled into the parking lot and headed inside the store, and was just headed over to the deli section when he ran into Rick Maroney looking at two packages of crackers like he couldn't decide between them.

"Oh, hey, Braden," Rick said, looking up at him.

The two men didn't know each other that well, but Rick was engaged to Darla, who was friends with Monica, so...

Braden almost blushed when he realized he was thinking of Monica as though she was his girlfriend, and hoped he hid his expression before Rick saw anything.

"How're you doing, Rick?"

Rick held up the two boxes in his hands. "Darla told me to buy the rosemary crackers, but these both have rosemary, so I'm trying to decide which one looks more like the kind we usually have, based on the picture on the front. It's not like she'll be mad if I get it wrong, but she's had a busy week, so I'd like to check this off her list, you know?"

Braden nodded, feeling oddly jealous. What would it be like to have the kind of established relationship where Monica sent *him* on errands when her week was busy? He shook his head at himself. He really was far gone over her if he was fantasizing about going to the grocery store.

Rick must have noticed his far-off look because he lowered both boxes into his cart and asked, "Everything okay?"

Braden almost didn't open up to Rick, but then he remembered something he had heard about when Rick and Darla first started dating. "When you and Darla first got together, she was living in New York, right?"

Rick's mouth twisted. "Kind of. Things started up between us while she was here for her grandmother's funeral, but then we split when she went back to New York. She came back though, and we've been together ever since. Why do you ask?"

"Nothing is official between us for now, but I've been getting closer to Monica."

Rick nodded. "Darla mentioned something to that effect," he admitted. "I think she and Marty both are rooting for you guys."

Braden couldn't help but smile. He knew what Monica would say. *The Whale Harbor gossip mill strikes again.*

"Well, in our situation, I'm kind of the Darla. I

used to work in Washington D.C., and I thought I would only be coming back to Whale Harbor for a short time. But I don't know, man... I can't stop thinking about her. Every time I see her, I only like her more. I talked to Thomas, and he reminded me I had to be careful, since Monica's last boyfriend was such a jerk. I guess I was hoping I could just get another perspective on things—one from someone a little closer to my age," he added with a chuckle.

Rick laughed too. "You're right in that I'm definitely more like Monica in this story—except for the terrible ex-boyfriend part. I knew I was staying in Whale Harbor and I couldn't imagine doing long-distance. Not because I didn't love Darla, but because I loved her so much. I don't think I could have lived with only getting her in little snippets of time."

Braden nodded. That sounded horrible.

Rick continued. "I can't tell you what it was like to decide to stay here—like I said, that wasn't my side of the story. But what I can tell you is that going all-in with Darla is the best decision I ever made. I have my professional ambitions like the next person, and so does she. But when you find the person you're meant to be with? All that other stuff is just noise. Being with Darla? That's the good stuff. That's the important part. Every day that I get to go home to her is amazing. It never gets old."

Listening to the simple, happy way Rick talked about his relationship with Darla made Braden's chest grow tight. The way Rick phrased things made it all sound so simple. And suddenly Braden found that it *was* simple.

He could be happy in Whale Harbor if he got to go home to Monica every night. It was a great little town and if things started to feel too little, well, that was what vacations and weekend trips were for. Besides, he wanted to continue to spend time with his mother regularly and—though he knew he was getting *way* ahead of himself here—he knew his mother would make the greatest grandmother in the world and would want to be near her grandkids every day. He even liked working on the fishing boat more than he had expected... though he'd never get used to those early wakeups, he was pretty sure.

Brimming with excitement, Braden clapped Rick on the shoulder. "Thanks, man. That's really great advice."

"You're welcome. I gotta say, I hope it works out for you and Monica. Mon is a great girl, and it'll really make Darla happy to see her happy, which means I'm invested too."

"I really hope it works out too," Braden replied.

He bid Rick farewell, leaving the man to continue puzzling over his cracker boxes, and went to go buy his dinner, planning all the while. Now that he had decided to pursue his future with Monica, he wanted to figure out a way to make that happen soon. He had to show her he could be careful with her feelings, but how? On the other hand, he had to make sure he wasn't being *too* careful. He didn't want her to think he wasn't serious about her when he definitely was. She was the most incredible woman he'd ever met, and it was important that she knew just how much he cared for her.

She deserved something special, he decided as he paid for his food and headed back to the car. Something that showcased his intentions *and* showed that he could be trusted with her recently bruised heart. As he drove home, he began working on his plan...

CHAPTER TWENTY-THREE

The library closed early on Mondays, so Monica decided to take advantage of her free afternoon by getting a few hours of work in at the B&B. One of the other librarians had been out sick, so she'd had less time than usual during the past few days to do much more than stop by and check on progress. Part of her was grateful for the distraction. She wasn't sure she was ready to see Braden yet, given the feelings she was wrestling with. She'd seen him here and there, of course—you couldn't go long in a town the size of Whale Harbor without running in to just about everyone—but their interactions had been more waving from a distance than having any intense conversations.

The whole time, however, she had been thinking about their situation and about what Marty had said at their lunch. Talking to her friend had made Monica realize that she'd spent so much time worrying about what could go *wrong* between her and Braden that she hadn't taken any time to focus on what could go *right* between them. Reorienting her thinking had helped clarify things, had made her feel ready to take a chance on what could be an incredible relationship, if only she stopped fearing the risk to her heart. Now she just had to figure out how to tell Braden how she felt.

That was the part that left her stuck. She'd been holding him at arm's length for a while, and though he'd been really understanding, she didn't want to assume that he felt as ready as she did to try for a relationship. Thinking that he might be made excited butterflies flutter in her tummy. Thinking that he might not be? Well... that caused her tummy to rumble with a much more unpleasant case of nerves. Even though she was worried about their next encounter, Monica felt disappointed when she pulled up to the B&B and realized his car wasn't there—or in the back, which she always checked after they had spooked one another that late night.

A little more time to decide what you're going to say isn't a bad thing, she reminded herself as she approached the front door. After a week of hard work, the bones of the porch were starting to take shape. It would be a while before anyone could enjoy a leisurely afternoon there, but she could see her dream starting to take shape—which filled her right back up with the good butterflies.

To Monica's surprise, there were flowers sitting on the table in the entryway. Marty had helped her find the antique piece of furniture, and it looked perfect but it had still been in storage when Monica had last left the B&B. Frowning in confusion, she picked up the note leaning against the vase of beautiful daffodils, which were looking cheerful and bright even though it was still only early spring.

Monica, she read, the blocky architect's handwriting already revealing Braden as the writer.

When I came back to Whale Harbor, I expected a lot of things, some that came true and some that didn't. I expected to grow closer with my mom, and I'll forever be grateful that this one falls in the 'came true' column. I expected to hate fishing and the early mornings, and I was surprised to learn that I don't. (Well, okay... maybe I do *hate the early mornings.) I expected to miss city life way more than I actually do. But whether or not they ended up how I expected, those things were all things I could imagine. They were the little changes.*

Then there were the big, unexpected changes. I never expected to get to see my mom fall in love again, and I never thought I would like her partner as much as I like Thomas. I never thought I would appreciate seeing the sun rise over the ocean the way that I do. I never thought you would see me in the ocean in March in New England!

But the biggest thing I never saw coming was you. You, Monica Grey, have totally knocked me off my feet. I've never met anyone like you, and I know I never will again. Who else could light up like the sun when talking about book-themed wallpaper and be brave enough to chase after her dreams and go toe-to-toe—or is it board-to-board?—with me in a surf competition?

I don't want you to think I'm taking this lightly. I've been thinking a lot, and I know you've been through a lot lately too. I talked to Thomas—who, it turns out, is great at advice—and he helped me understand what it means to care about someone who had their heart broken. But he assured me that it's possible to find happiness and love again—and he would know, because he and my mom eloped this week!

Monica gasped as she read that part.

I think if the two of them can find love again after losing their spouses, the letter continued, *that we owe it to ourselves to take a chance too. But I can be patient. I'm not going anywhere. You're worth waiting for.*

If you're ready to talk about it, I'll be waiting at the beach tonight at 5pm. You know the place. I hope I'll see you there.

Yours,

Braden

When she was done reading, Monica had tears in her eyes. She wiped hastily at her cheeks. If she hadn't already been certain that she wanted to try with Braden, that letter would have made her sure. So many things he had written made her sure that he was the one for her. It wasn't only the things he had said about caring for her, but the way he talked about his mother and new stepdad, the way he admitted the things he'd been wrong about, and the way he was willing to patiently wait for her only reinforced what she'd already known. Braden was nothing like Connor. He wouldn't be careless with her heart.

She looked around her beautiful B&B, at this dream that Braden was helping her build. This was her new start—not just her business, but for her heart too. This was her chance to be brave and take a chance on love. She grinned to herself, her heart racing.

Then something occurred to her and she glanced at her watch. Shoot! It was already well past four thirty. She had to hurry to make it to the beach on time.

As she hurried back to her car and got behind the wheel, she thought of one line of Braden's letter. *I'm not going anywhere.* She hoped that meant what she thought it did.

Braden had been pacing back and forth for so long that he had worn a little divot in the sand. Frowning, he glanced down at it and kicked some sand into the hole. It was one thing to be nervous about Monica's decision to meet him, and it was quite another thing to ruin his romantic gesture by tripping and breaking his ankle in a hole he'd made himself.

He glanced over at the picnic blanket he'd set up, which was illuminated with torches he'd stuck into the sand, which provided both light and a little warmth. On the ground was a large, soft blanket, where he'd laid out gourmet turkey sandwiches made with a slathering of pesto on thick slices of artisanal bread, tiny quiches in self-contained little pie crusts, and berry cobbler, complete with ice cream staying cold in the ice bucket where a bubbly bottle of rosé sat chilling. Braden was a decent cook, but he wasn't afraid to admit that he had purchased this premade from the Clownfish Eatery. Gourmet foods were a little outside his comfort zone, but he wanted to make a big gesture for Monica.

He looked up and his heart leaped when he saw the woman in question coming down into the little cove. She wore a huge smile that made hope catch in Braden's throat. Did that mean... ?

She was hurrying toward him, and he started moving toward her, as well, before his brain even realized what his feet were doing. When they met in the middle, she threw her arms around his neck in a huge, exuberant hug. He pressed his face against her soft blonde hair, feeling more complete now that she was in his arms. After a long, tight embrace, she pulled back.

"What's all this?" She gestured at the picnic. "I thought you asked me down here to talk."

He grinned, tugging at her hand to pull her over to the blanket. "Well, I do want to talk, but I also wanted to do it in style. You deserve a big gesture and I really wanted to show you how I feel."

Her smile was so pretty he felt like he could look at it forever. "You already did a big gesture. I loved the letter and the flowers."

"Pshaw." Braden mimed brushing off his shoulders. "You think that's romance? You just wait until I bring my A-game, Grey. You're not going to know what hit you."

She laughed and bumped him with her shoulder. He used the opportunity to wrap his arm around her. When he looked down into her wide, trusting eyes, he grew serious.

"I mean everything I said in the letter, Mon. I'll wait as long as you need. There's no need to rush. But I want you to know—I'm all in. As long as you will have me, I'll be here. In Whale Harbor. With you."

She gasped, both of her hands flying to her mouth. "You're staying?" she asked, voice small but hopeful.

He nodded. "When I thought about it, I realized I was being silly. I was letting something that might *potentially* make me unhappy in the future prevent me from pursuing something that would *definitely* make me happy in the present. I want a relationship with you and I want us to build a life here together—whenever you're ready," he added hastily, not wanting her to think he was going back on his word not to rush her.

He needn't have worried, however, because Monica threw her arms around his neck again, this time planting a kiss right on his mouth. Braden wrapped his arms around her waist, kissing her with all the feeling that he held in his heart. They held each other for a few minutes, enjoying the feeling of being together.

Eventually, Monica pulled back with a laugh. "In case you didn't realize, that means yes! I want us to be together too, and I don't want to wait."

"I kind of figured," he said. They were both still laughing when they pulled together to kiss again.

He was pretty sure he'd never get tired of kissing her, but the food was waiting, so they sat down to eat. Conversation had always flowed well between them, but with their feelings out in the open, things were even easier.

"I'm going to have to decide a bit more formally how to divide my contracting time and my fishing time," he mused as they ate their sandwiches. "So far, I've just been building things whenever people needed them, but I'll have to plan a bit more for the long term. I'm hoping the finest B&B proprietress will hire me on as a handyman though."

"I'll put in a good word for you," she teased with a wink.

The more Braden thought about it, the more he liked the idea of sticking with the kind of contracting work he had been doing around Whale Harbor.

"I think there will be enough work for me here, and I'm really excited to be building on my own terms, with things I'm in charge of. Back at my old firm, it was never just me and the client trying to work out where our visions aligned. There were always a million other people who had to sign off on anything before the work could begin."

She pretended to be shocked. "And you, Braden Watson, had a problem with that? Are you implying you were stubborn?"

"Hush, you." He threw a berry at her. She popped it in her mouth. "Maybe I'm a bit stubborn, but I'm learning to be more flexible, learning to see where life takes me instead of focusing so intently on where I always thought I wanted to go. And, I have to say, I'm liking that approach." He gestured around them as if to say, *Look where it got me.*

Monica leaned forward to clink glasses—though it didn't make the traditional sound, since glass wasn't allowed on the beach and their wine glasses were plastic.

"I'm glad you ended up where you are," she said.

He reached forward to tuck a strand of hair that had been tugged loose by the ocean breeze back behind her ear. "It wasn't a direct path for either of us, but I'm so grateful that we both found our way here."

They shifted closer to kiss again, their mouths tasting of berries and pink wine.

They chatted for so long, the conversation easily shifting from one topic to the next, that the sun had fully gone down before Braden realized he had forgotten something.

"Oh no," he cried, smacking himself in the forehead. "I completely forgot—I planned a sunset surf for us, but now we missed it."

Monica shifted closer to him until she was snuggled up under his arm, giggling at his show of disappointment. "That's okay. We have as many sunset surfs as we want in our future."

He was happy to raise a glass to that. As he

tapped his glass to hers again, he couldn't be sorry about plans they had missed, not when their future was so bright. As the torches burned down around him, he looked down at her with a grin, wondering if his heart had ever felt so light.

CHAPTER TWENTY-FOUR

Braden delicately shaved down the edge of a door at the B&B. Monica had mentioned it was sticking—which made sense for old wood in an ocean town like theirs—so he wanted to fix it for her before he went back to the bigger project of finishing the deck railing.

He caught himself grinning as he worked. That had been happening a lot lately, he thought with a rueful shake of his head. But who could blame him? The last few weeks had been some of the happiest of his life.

Ever since that night on the beach, he and Monica had spent nearly every day together. Even though she had to spend some of her time at the library and he had to juggle the B&B repairs with the other projects he had been hired to do around town, they always came together at some point, whether it was for dinner, to work companionably on the B&B, or to slip over to 'their' beach for a quick surf. Things just felt so *right* between them. He had thought the connection between them was strong before, but now that they had let go of their old fears enough to stop holding back, he felt closer to her than ever. Just thinking about her filled his chest with a warm feeling—the kind of feeling it was probably too soon to be experiencing, let alone say out loud.

He was just finishing up sanding down the door's edge—it would need to be repainted before the B&B opened, but at least now they could go through it more easily—when Monica came down the stairs, blowing a wisp of blonde hair out of her face. The warm feeling grew at the sight of her.

"I just can't visualize it," she said, tone mildly irritated. "I think I need to put some furniture in there first. Any chance you'd like to go to Blueberry Bay with me?"

She had been upstairs, working on the section of the B&B where she would live. While she had a clear vision for the business parts of her building, Braden knew she had been struggling a little with deciding how to arrange the little apartment of rooms where she would live.

"Of course," he said in response to her invitation. "Let me just finish up here." He waved a hand at his tools.

Blueberry Bay was the next town over, but because the B&B sat on one edge of Whale Harbor, the Blueberry Bay town limits were technically only about a block away. Since she would be operating her business on the cusp of two towns, he knew that Monica wanted to patronize a furniture store in Blueberry Bay—despite her loyalty to Marty. When Monica had expressed her feelings of disloyalty to Marty when they had had dinner with her and Wyatt a few nights before, Marty had laughed and promised Monica she was not offended.

Braden packed away his tools as Monica ducked into one of the recently finished bathrooms to tidy her hair.

"Oh, I've been meaning to tell you!" She poked her head out of the bathroom, hands still smoothing her ponytail. Her words were muffled by the hair tie between her teeth, so he grabbed it and held it for her. "Thanks. Anyway, I wanted to tell you—I was out for an early morning walk the other day, and I found this perfect little spot on the beach. I think we should go over there for a surf whenever we next get the time."

"Sounds great to me." Everything sounded great when he did it with her. "You know, one of the first things I liked about you was that you have both a bookish side and an outdoorsy side. I just love that you love surfing." It felt dangerous to use the 'l-word' about her, but in a good way. The warm chest feeling pulsed at the thought.

She grinned at him as they headed toward the door. "Well, I'm glad you like book nerds—because I definitely am one."

He threw an arm around her shoulders. It felt amazing that this was something he could do so casually now. "I think the book wallpaper gave you away on that one," he teased. "But don't worry—I like all the sides of you."

She pressed up onto her toes and gave him a quick peck on the cheek.

The drive to the antique store only took them a few minutes. They chattered happily, talking about the new mystery Braden was reading and the dinner they planned to have with Thomas and Gabrielle soon. The shop was very different from Marty's calming, curated store. Blueberry Bay Antiquities was the kind of place where you had to hunt for the treasures that might be hiding behind a tangle of old furniture.

Normally, this wasn't Braden's favorite activity. He preferred the architecture side of things, the big picture elements of building, over the smaller details of decorating. But he found himself having a great time as he trailed behind Monica as she poked through the haphazard stacks of things in no discernible order, bantering with her about who they thought the original owners were for items like a teeny tiny rocking chair or a spool of thread that was at least two feet tall.

Watching her face as she carefully considered the comfort of a plush antique bench she was considering buying, he thought of something his mother had said once when he'd teased her that she seemed excited to go to the grocery store with Thomas.

"Oh, honey." She had laughed, shaking her head at him. "When everything's fun—that's how you know you've found 'the one.'"

At the time, he had thought his mother was just being silly, but now that he looked at Monica as she bounced gently on the ancient springs of the chaise, he thought that maybe he understood what his mother had meant.

* * *

Darla checked her appearance one last time before she headed out the front door. It was officially the opening of the museum, and she felt like she was about to burst with excitement and nerves. Today was a little open house with snacks, drinks, and other activities for families and kids so that Whale Harbor could get a taste of how the museum could benefit their community.

"You look perfect," Rick called from behind her. "Just like you did last time you checked."

She rolled her eyes—at herself, not at her fiancé. "I know, I know. I just can't get my nerves to calm down, and for some reason that's popping into my head as the worry that I'll have a great big clown smear of lipstick on my face."

He appeared next to her reflection in the mirror. "How about this? I promise that if you start to look even the *tiniest* bit like a clown, I'll give you this signal." He did a complicated hand gesture that was not the least bit subtle, making Darla laugh, as he had no doubt intended.

"Deal," she agreed. "And thanks for taking off work today to be here with me. I can't even imagine how nervous I would be if you weren't here."

"Are you kidding? There's no place I'd rather be." He hugged her from behind and she leaned into the warmth of his embrace. His reassuring smile as he met her gaze made her heart thump with how much she cared for him.

"I love you, Rick," she said, putting all her feeling into the words.

"I love you too, Madam Curator. Now, let's head over to the museum so I can bask in how cool and accomplished my amazing fiancée is."

Darla turned in his arms, reaching up to kiss him, but at the last minute he pulled back, a twinkle in his eye.

"What about your fears about getting clown mouth?" he joked.

She put both hands on his face, holding him still as she planted a big smacking kiss on his mouth. "Worth it."

She did, however, check her lipstick one last time before they walked out their front door.

Even with Rick's reassurances, her nerves spiked as they headed to the museum, so Darla was pleased when Marty and her mom arrived only a few minutes after the open house officially began.

"Oh my gosh!" Marty exclaimed before she was

even all the way through the door. "Look at this place, Dar! This is incredible."

This compliment meant a lot coming from her sister, who had an impeccable eye for design, but Darla was more anxious to hear what Lori thought. Their relationship had come a long way since Darla had returned to Whale Harbor and they'd discussed everything that had stood between them for so long, but this project was really dear to Darla, and she was a tad worried over what her mom would think. Her nerves spiked even higher when Lori was quiet for a long moment and then turned to her daughter, tears in her eyes.

"Oh no, Mom!" Darla exclaimed, alarm crashing through her. "What's wrong?"

"What's wrong?" Lori echoed. "Honey, nothing is wrong—this is *amazing*."

Darla's concern quickly transformed into relief as her mom kept talking.

"I'm so proud of you I could burst, sweetie. And then I start to think of all the years I didn't support you and your art, and I realize how silly I was to think that you would live your life making exactly the choices I would make. And I hate how much I hurt you with that attitude—"

"Mom!" Darla interrupted, rushing forward to

embrace Lori. "All that is in the past. We've already talked about it, and you know that everything is forgiven. I don't want to hear you worrying about that anymore."

Lori sniffled a little. "Okay, if you insist. But... I'm still allowed to brag about how proud of you I am, right? Because that kind of thing is very important to a mother."

Darla laughed, opening her arms to include Marty, who had stepped closer to be included in the hug. "Yeah, Mom, that part is okay with me."

The three women embraced until Marty couldn't contain her excitement anymore and demanded that Darla show her everything. They moved through the exhibits in detail, Marty and Lori *ooh*ing and *aah*ing over all of Darla's choices and asking engaged questions. Darla felt grateful that she got to practice her answers on a friendly audience, but when time inched forward and it was still just the four of them—Rick having rejoined the group after leaving the Sims women to their special moment—Darla began to worry nobody else would show up.

"Do you think this is going to be it?" Darla fretted, twisting her champagne flute between her fingers. This was a daytime event and there were activities for kids too, so it was only sparkling water in the glass, but the motion soothed her. "Do you think I didn't advertise enough?"

Her family didn't even get a chance to reassure her before the door burst open and Lucas, Charity's son, entered, dragging his mother behind him.

"C'mon, Mom!" he urged. "We don't want to miss anything!"

Charity appeared next, laughing at her son's exuberance. "We won't, we won't! Look, you're the first kid here."

"Cool!" exclaimed Lucas. He immediately spotted the kids area and rushed over to explore. Rick followed so that Charity could say hello to her friends without worrying about her son's supervision.

Charity had barely finished her preliminary glance around when the door opened again, this time admitting Monica and Braden—who were, Darla noticed with a grin at her friends, holding hands. She had heard through the Whale Harbor grapevine that the pair had finally gotten out of their own way and decided to be together, but she had been so busy with the museum that she hadn't yet seen them together. They approached to echo Charity's admiring comments about the museum.

After that, the trickle of people turned into a

flood. Gabrielle and Thomas Watson-Thermond—the couple had decided to hyphenate, since they wanted to share a last name and honor the family they already had, including their late spouses—arrived in a haze of newlywed bliss.

Rose and Darell Smith came, as did Jordan, Rick's coworker from the marine center, accompanied by a number of men Darla vaguely knew from the docks. Many of these men stopped over to talk with Braden. Eventually, the crowd got so big that Darla could only pay attention to the people immediately in front of her, although she spotted several of her mother's friends, several of the families and students she knew from school, and even a few people she didn't recognize, suggesting they might not even be from Whale Harbor.

She talked for so long that her throat felt dry and smiled so much that her cheeks hurt. Rick appeared at her elbow, holding a glass of water, which Darla sipped gratefully.

"Was it everything you wanted?" he asked quietly as people milled around them.

Despite her aching cheeks, she couldn't help the grin that split her face. "Everything and more. It's even better than my art show in New York because this whole project is mine. It feels like an ode to art, or a love letter to my passion." She winked at Rick, thinking of the love letters he had written her.

"And it's home," he added. He knew her so well.

"Exactly."

As they stood together, looking out over the crowd, Darla silently acknowledged that sharing her passion with the people of Whale Harbor meant more to her than she ever could have imagined.

CHAPTER TWENTY-FIVE

"Hello!" Marty called as she entered through the front door of Monica's B&B. The place was really starting to look amazing, evidence of her friend's hard work and Braden's expertise as a contractor. The hardwood floors had all been refinished, and the faintest smell of paint hung in the air from the freshly redone walls, although Marty knew that all the windows Monica currently had open would swiftly do away with what remained of the odor.

"In here!"

She followed Monica's voice—and the smell of freshly-baked cookies, which grew stronger as she approached the kitchen—glancing at each room as she went, marveling at the potential of each space.

Monica had done a beautiful job already, blending soothing neutral colors with bright pops of color that kept the space from looking monochrome or boring, and Marty's mind raced with ideas on how to make each room as comfortable and lovely as possible for Monica's future guests.

Monica was in the kitchen, pulling a tray full of what smelled like oatmeal raisin cookies out of the oven.

"Those smell *amazing,*" Marty said, putting down her bag, which contained samples and design catalogues, before embracing Monica. "If this is how the B&B is going to smell, I'm going to stay here myself, never mind that I live five minutes down the road."

Monica laughed. "Oh, man, wait until you taste them before you make any promises. I've been trying to tweak my recipe, and I'm not sure if this batch turned out just right." She shuffled the cookies onto a wire cooling rack as she explained. "I'm not planning on doing all the cooking myself, since that's a full-time job all on its own, but I do want to have some fresh cookies to greet guests. I'm thinking of offering oatmeal raisin and chocolate chip. I asked Charity for some tips about making big batches and freezing the dough so it's ready when I need it, and I'm testing things out now."

Marty grabbed a cookie from the cooling rack, juggling it between her hands for a few moments until it was cool enough to bite into. "Oh, yeah," she mumbled around her mouthful, not even caring that it wasn't exactly the best manners. "It's official. I'm moving in. One of these rooms we're decorating is for me and Wyatt, right?"

"I think your cats might have something to say about going from a full house to one room."

She took another bite of the cookie before answering. "Peaches can be the B&B mascot. With enough guests, she'll finally get the adoration she deserves."

The two women laughed at the mental image of Peaches strutting around the B&B, eyeballing everyone who didn't give her enough pets. Monica piled some cookies onto a plate and poured them two glasses of cold milk to go with their snack as Marty pulled out her design materials.

"I don't want every room to match, exactly," Monica explained as she looked through what Marty had brought. "But I do want there to be... well, cohesion, I guess. So that way if people come back for repeat visits, they get to have the same atmosphere without feeling like they're in a big, corporate hotel."

"Absolutely." Marty rifled through the pile until she found the samples she was looking for. "What if we did something like this?" She indicated a spread that showed different pieces of furniture, all made from the same type of wood and with similar thematic elements, even while each individual piece was different.

"Ooh," Monica cooed, pulling the magazine toward her. "I love that."

They spent a while going over different furniture options, textures to enhance the cozy feel of each room, and color schemes to make each room feel unique without detracting from the overall ambiance of the B&B. Marty mostly listened, using Monica's vision as their primary guide, providing little suggestions here and there. As they worked, Marty couldn't help but think how much this affirmed her decision to stay in Whale Harbor. Working at Sharp's would have been amazing, but there was no way working for a big company with fancy clients would have been as satisfying as seeing a friend make her dream come true in Marty's very own hometown.

By the time they were done working, the plate of

cookies was empty. Monica poured them cups of coffee—decaf, since it was getting late in the afternoon—and they moved into the front sitting room, where plush armchairs had recently been installed.

"Ooh, I love this," Marty said, running her fingers over the velveteen texture of the chair before sitting down. "It feels cozy and luxe at the same time. And comfortable!" she added once she was seated.

Monica, seated in her own chair, wiggled happily. "Aren't they great? Braden and I found them at that antiques store in Blueberry Bay."

Marty took a sip of her coffee as she gave her friend a knowing glance over the rim of her mug. "Well, now that you mention him, how are things going with Braden? Spill!"

Monica blushed, but it was an expression of happiness, not embarrassment. "Things between us are just so wonderful! It makes me feel silly for letting my old fears hold me back for so long."

"Oh, hush," Marty chided gently. "Hindsight is twenty-twenty, isn't that what they say? You'd been hurt before. It was natural that you'd want to avoid being hurt again."

Monica smiled. "Thanks. Braden was really supportive too. And now that we're past that it's amazing. We've been spending basically every day together."

"Sounds like it's getting serious."

The cheerful blush returned. "It is. I think—" She hesitated, then lowered her voice as if she was confessing a secret. "I think he might be my forever person."

"Honey!" Marty exclaimed with a laugh. She took Monica's mug from her hands and put both cups down on a side table so she could wrap her friend in a hug. "Don't say it like that! That's amazing!"

Monica pulled back. She too, was laughing. "I know, I know. It's just still pretty new, so I don't want to get ahead of myself. It doesn't feel like there's a rush though. It feels like we have all the time in the world."

"That's how you know it's right," Marty told her.

They chatted for a little while longer before Wyatt arrived to pick Marty up for their quad riding date, which they had scheduled for that evening. At the door to the B&B, Monica hugged her goodbye.

"Thanks for all the help! I couldn't have done it without you."

Marty brushed off the compliment. "You could

have... but probably not as well," she teased. Monica laughed.

"Definitely not. Okay, go have your date with that handsome fiancé of yours."

Marty beamed. It still felt fresh and exciting to call Wyatt her fiancé.

As she headed out to meet him, she couldn't help but think how proud she felt—of herself, of her friend, and of her town.

* * *

Monica put her hands on her hips and looked at the placement of the very last piece of art she had to hang, in one of the rear bedrooms on the second floor of the B&B. The dreamy landscape, done by a local artist that Darla had connected her to, looked perfect above the armchair. Every bedroom had a comfy place to read, so that guests could curl up with a book either in the public spaces or in the comfort of their own rooms.

She left the room and trailed through the B&B, trying to look at it objectively. Between Marty's advice, her own hard work, and Braden's contracting experience, Monica thought everything had turned out amazingly well. *This might be a small-town establishment,* she thought to herself with satisfaction, *but I think even any big-city guests would be more than satisfied.*

She wandered into the front room and looked out the big window. Braden was on the front porch, touching up some of the weatherproofing varnish on one of the railings. He had technically finished this part of the project the other day, but just as he had called her out to look at everything, a bird had landed right on the spot he'd just finished working on, leaving little birdie footprints behind. They'd laughed so hard they'd had to sit down.

The memory, as well as the easy, comfortable way he moved around the space made Monica think, not for the first time, how much Braden was so unlike Connor. Connor never would have laughed if a bird messed up his work. He would have sulked and pouted, wanting Monica to fix things for him. Braden, however, had shrugged in a *that's life* sort of way and touched up the spot when he got a chance. She was so lucky to have him, she thought as she watched him step back and assess his work with his hands on his hips, just like she had done upstairs only a few minutes before. He was her best friend and her future, and she was filled with gratitude that he had waited for her to get past her unfounded fears.

Thinking about how wonderful they were together made her want to be with him without a window between them, so she headed outside, stopping first in the kitchen to grab them each a glass of lemonade.

He turned around as soon as she stepped out onto the porch.

"Well, well," he said, face lighting up with a smile. "If it isn't the prettiest B&B owner in the world."

She laughed. "You keep saying that."

"It keeps being true." He accepted the offered glass of lemonade. "Thanks. It's already starting to warm up out here. Feels like it was winter just yesterday, but we're well into spring now, aren't we?"

She nodded, feeling herself fill up with both excitement and trepidation. The grand opening of the B&B was scheduled for Memorial Day, since that was a weekend when a lot of people traveled. She still had a little bit of time—but she also still had a lot to do.

When she returned to the present moment, stepping away from her mental to-do list, she caught Braden watching her fondly.

"Nerves?" he asked.

She rolled her eyes at herself. "Gosh, you know me so well."

He wrapped an arm around her shoulders and led her to the porch swing he had installed the week prior. They nestled together into the cushions and rocked gently, Braden propelling them lightly with one foot on the ground.

"Want to talk about it?" he asked.

She took a sip of her lemonade. "It's nothing new, I'm afraid. We've done all this work and it's amazing, but this last part—whether people like it, whether they tell their friends or want to come back —that feels out of my hands, you know?" She twisted her mouth a little. "I think I'm going to be nervous until we actually get past the opening part. Sorry about that."

"Hey." He placed their lemonade glasses on the ground and turned to face her, expression serious. "Don't apologize about that. I want to hear about all your thoughts and feelings—even the bad ones, or the silly ones. I want to know when you're scared or anxious or sad so that I can remind you that, no matter what happens, I'll be by your side."

He made the declaration so earnestly, as if it were just that simple. The honest affection in his words touched her deeply. This feeling of support was the opposite of how she had felt with Connor. In her past relationship, she had always tried to be upbeat and bubbly, so she didn't add to Connor's stress. She hadn't realized until this moment how hard that had been for her. But Braden had realized it and had reached out a helping hand without her even having to ask.

As she looked at him, taking in his kind, handsome face, and his easy, affectionate smile, she felt the feeling bubble up inside her, felt the truth coming out before she could stop it.

"I love you, Braden," she said.

Instantly, his eyes widened, and she worried it was too soon. Maybe she shouldn't have said anything?

But then his smile got bigger. "I love you too, Monica."

Her grin was as big as his. "Phew! I was worried there for a second that I'd scared you off."

He chuckled. "Would you believe that *I* was scared to say anything in case I scared *you* off?"

"You know?" she said, leaning in to kiss him softly. "I would. Because, as it turns out, we're a perfect match."

"Cheers to that," he said, handing her back her lemonade so they could clink glasses.

They settled back on the swing as the afternoon faded into evening and Monica found that she could picture a future that looked just like this: her and Braden, happy and together.

CHAPTER TWENTY-SIX

In the middle of May, Monica held a "soft opening" for her B&B, an idea Darla had provided after the success of her open house for the museum. Darla had seen her friend grow increasingly nervous as the date for her first paying guests' arrival approached and had floated the idea one day when she and Monica were out to brunch with Rick, Braden, Marty, and Wyatt. Although the three men weren't quite as close of friends as the women yet, they had begun to bond, mostly over playful arguments over what was better: fishing—which Rick and Braden defended—or quad racing—Wyatt's opinion, of course. Braden had turned away from his concession that, admittedly, quad racing benefitted from not having to get up at four in the morning to do it, to chime in on Darla's idea.

"You know," he said to Monica, beaming like he did every time he looked at his girlfriend. "My mom and Thomas never got to have a local celebration for their wedding. I bet they would love to do that at the B&B, so you can get in a trial event before the big day."

"Ooh, yes, do that," Marty added. "That way I can maybe steal some wedding ideas from them."

"You don't have any ideas?" Monica was shocked. "But you're such an amazing designer!"

Marty put her hands to her face in mock horror. "There are just so many things to plan! But you wait and see," she said, wagging a finger between Monica and Braden. "It'll be your turn, soon enough."

Darla was afraid her sister had embarrassed their friend, whose relationship was still relatively new, but Monica merely smiled to herself, and Braden wrapped his arm around her shoulders, looking pleased as punch.

"I think your sister is right," Rick commented on their way home later that afternoon. "I bet those two don't waste any time deciding to get married. They have that look."

"When you know, you know," Darla said, smiling at her own 'forever person' as he drove them back home.

Thomas and Gabrielle ended up loving the idea of having a belated wedding celebration and had planned a fun-filled barbecue to take place on the B&B's porch and lawn. The event was catered by The Blue Crab, with food preparation assisted by Monica's newly hired B&B chef, a no-nonsense woman in her sixties named Maureen who, according to Monica, ruled the kitchen with an iron fist.

Darla sipped a glass of raspberry lemonade, complete with a garnish on the side and a cute little paper straw, as she watched some of the local kids, including Charity's son, Lucas, play an energetic game of freeze-tag... along with Rick and Wyatt, who played with as much vigor as any of the children.

Her eyes drifted over to the porch, where Monica and Braden looked out over the event, which was going off without a hitch. She wondered if they even realized that they were leaning toward one another, as if there were just a natural magnetic force drawing them together.

"Well, aren't those two in their own little world of joy?"

Darla turned to see her mom come up beside her and nod at Monica and Braden.

"Hey, Mom!" She gave Lori a one-armed hug, then followed the line of her mom's gaze. "Yeah, they look insanely happy, don't they? I'm so excited for them as they get started on this next chapter."

Lori nodded. "They make a great couple. And, if I do say so myself, I had a hand in it."

"Oh, yeah?" Darla laughed. "How do you figure?"

Lori huffed, like it should have been obvious. "Well, I sold her the building, didn't I? And then she hired him to fix the place up. And then boom!" Lori clapped her hands together. "Love. I'm basically a fairy godmother."

"That's pretty romantic, coming from you, Mom. Does this mean you're thinking about romance in your future?"

Lori looked at her daughter as though Darla had just suggested that Lori give up being a realtor to join the circus. "Don't be silly, sweetheart. You know me. Both feet planted firmly on the ground. Besides," she huffed. "I'm too old to change."

Darla bumped shoulders with her mom. "You're not old at all," she chided. She decided not to bring up the other part. She didn't want to push her mom before she was ready, but seeing how happy Gabrielle and Thomas were with their later-in-life marriage, Darla was even more determined to see her mom just as happy, as well. Her mom could be stubborn, but Darla was patient.

Mother and daughter stood around chatting for a while, until some of Lori's friends waved her over. Darla waved her off, telling her mom she would catch up with her later, and looked around, just enjoying the ambiance of a beautiful spring day and the universal happiness that electrified the air.

Or... the *near* universal happiness, she realized as she spotted Charity, standing off to the side of the revelry, worrying her lower lip between her teeth. With a frown, Darla approached her friend to check in.

"Hey, honey! Everything okay?" she greeted her friend affectionately.

At Darla's approach, Charity looked up and pasted a smile on her face, but it didn't reach her eyes. "Oh, yeah, of course. Beautiful party, isn't it? I'm so happy for Thomas and Gabrielle."

Something about Charity's voice was off, but her posture struck Darla as a bit guarded and defensive, indicating that this wasn't a good time to press the matter.

"Yeah, it's amazing." Darla paused, then said, "And just in case you hit a point where everything *isn't* okay, know that you've always got an ear to listen and a shoulder to lean on in me, okay?"

Charity shot her a *you know me so well* look out of the corner of her eye. "Thanks. I'm just muddling things over in my mind, but I promise that if I need a friend, I will absolutely come to you."

"That's all I ask." Darla linked arms with her friend. She opened her mouth to ask if Charity had tried the crab cakes, which were amazing, but Lucas ran over, cheeks flushed with excitement.

"Mom! Mom! You gotta come see! Mr. Rick found a bird's nest in the tree and he's lifting us up so we can look at it." He started to pull Charity away by the hand. "But you *can't* touch, because then the mama bird might not come back. Okay?"

"Okay." Charity laughed, letting Lucas pull her along. She looked over her shoulder at Darla. "Apparently that fiancé of yours is getting a workout today, lifting everybody up to look inside a tree."

She was gone before Darla could respond, leaving the other woman alone with her thoughts about how good a father Rick would make one day. She was caught up in these happy thoughts as Marty came up to stand beside her.

"Heya, sis," Marty said cheerfully. "Having fun?"

"Of course!" Darla waved a hand. "Who wouldn't be with a party like this?"

Marty nodded. "And such a beautiful setting too. And do you know what might be even *more* beautiful? The inside, where one intrepid local designer contributed lots of great ideas."

Darla laughed. "A *modest* intrepid local designer?"

"Exactly," Marty joked. "Now, I'm not naming any names but..."

The two sisters cracked up.

"Okay," said Darla, linking her arm with Marty's. "Show me this masterpiece."

As they headed inside, Darla couldn't help but think that this was a perfect day—and an auspicious launch for Monica's new life.

* * *

Even though they'd been married for weeks, Gabrielle and Thomas were shown out in a shower of birdseed, which the guests dutifully threw *away* from the porch after Braden, mock stern, reminded them that he had *just* finished painting the thing, and didn't need to invite a thousand birds to do their business all over his handiwork, thank you very much. The birds were brave too. One even tried to nab a piece of birdseed off Gabrielle's shoulder, which made the older woman laugh in delight.

"That has to be an omen of good luck, right?" she asked her husband, who shrugged.

"Couldn't say. I'm already the luckiest man in the world."

In response to that, Gabrielle had planted a kiss right on his mouth as the guests cheered and whistled.

Guests had started to head home after that, slowly trickling out after congratulating Monica on her new endeavor. Some of their close friends had stayed behind to help with cleanup—though Charity had left early, Lucas half-asleep on his feet after the exciting day of running around with other kids—until Monica had sent them home, as well, leaving her and Braden to wrap up the last details.

In the kitchen of the B&B, they wrapped up what was left of the food—which wasn't much, since everything had been so delicious—and loaded plates into the dishwasher. *Even chores became fun when you did it with someone you loved*, Monica thought happily.

"So, did today's 'trial run' make you feel better about the opening?" he asked as he scrubbed down a big serving platter that didn't fit in the dishwasher. His sleeves were rolled up to his elbows, a dish towel thrown over one shoulder, and she took a second to admire the sweet, domestic picture he painted before she replied.

"Way better. I talked to my supervisor, and she'll let me keep some hours at the library while things get off the ground here. I've cut back, of course, but that'll be a nice cushion for my peace of mind while everything gets going."

"I bet it won't take long," Braden said with the confidence of a man in love who knew in his heart that the woman he cared for could do anything. "You're going to be a huge success. I know it."

She laughed. "I think you might be biased. But there are already some bookings coming in, so I'm optimistic too."

"Pshaw," he scoffed, wiping the last dish, and turning off the water. He dried his hands on the dish towel. "Who wouldn't want to stay here? It's perfect."

Monica looked around at the building around

her, each detail lovingly chosen and painstakingly put into place. This was her labor of love, yes, but it was more than that, because there were touches of the other citizens of Whale Harbor everywhere. Marty had chosen the framed prints of fruit, for example, that hung over the butcher block counter. Lori had helped Monica get this building, and Darla had given her advice on how to plan an opening event. And, of course, Braden's touches were everywhere. He was built into the very bones of the building. This was Monica's business, but in many ways it was *their* project too. It told the story of their love coming to be.

"It is perfect, isn't it?" she asked.

"Well..." His voice came from behind her. "I could think of one way to make it a little more perfect."

Monica turned and then gasped when she saw Braden, down on one knee, holding a ring in front of him. It was a beautiful ring, a classic princess cut diamond set in white gold, but in that moment, she only had eyes for the man, not the item of jewelry he held.

"I know this is a little fast," he said, eyes shining and expression nervous. "And you don't have to say yes if you're not ready. But I never want you to doubt how I feel about you. You are the one for me, Monica Grey. I know it in my bones. So, for me, the timing doesn't matter, because once you know you've found the one, nothing else is important. So, my love, would you do me the honor of being my wife?"

Her heart racing, she looked down at him. It was just so like him, to acknowledge any fears she might have and reassure them even before they could fully appear in her mind. He had always done that, she realized, had always been honest and clear with her about what he wanted. Which meant, to her surprise, that her fears never came. It must be right, she knew, because she felt eager, rather than anxious, to take this leap.

"Yes!" she cried, tears of happiness springing to her eyes. "Yes, I'll marry you!"

Braden leapt to his feet and pulled her into his arms. He bent toward her for a kiss, then pulled back. "Whoops, wait, ring first," he said.

She laughed, holding out her finger. The ring fit perfectly, but she only admired it for a split second, because she couldn't wait one moment longer to kiss her fiancé. Her fiancé! Even the thought was exciting.

"Do you like it?" he asked, after they pulled

back. He held her hand in his as they gazed down at the ring. "We can get a different one if you don't—"

Monica gasped, snatching back her hand. "Don't you dare! I love it. And I love you," she added, tugging his head down for another kiss.

"You know what this means?" she asked him after they'd pulled away from one another and Braden had reached into the fridge to pull out a bottle of champagne to celebrate. "The B&B wasn't just *my* fresh start—it's *our* fresh start."

He looked around as he handed her a flute full of bubbly liquid. "Do you want to get married here? It's only the best place in Whale Harbor." He winked and she laughed.

"That sounds like a lot of work on top of being the bride."

"Bride," he echoed. "Boy, do I like the sound of that. You know, we could always take a page out of my mom and Thomas's book and elope."

He said it a bit offhandedly, but the more Monica thought about the idea, the more she liked it. The idea of a private ceremony, just the two of them and maybe a few close friends and family as witnesses, sounded amazing to her. Plus, it would save a lot of time.

"You know," she said. "I think we should. I don't

want to wait. It's like you said—when it's the right person, the timing doesn't matter. And I've never been so sure of anything in my life."

Braden's smile was so bright that it was nearly blinding as she pulled him in for a kiss.

ALSO BY FIONA BAKER

The Marigold Island Series

The Beachside Inn

Beachside Beginnings

Beachside Promises

Beachside Secrets

Beachside Memories

Beachside Weddings

Beachside Holidays

Beachside Treasures

The Sea Breeze Cove Series

The House by the Shore

A Season of Second Chances

A Secret in the Tides

The Promise of Forever

A Haven in the Cove

The Blessing of Tomorrow

A Memory of Moonlight

The Snowy Pine Ridge Series

The Christmas Lodge

Sweet Christmas Wish

Second Chance Christmas

Christmas at the Guest House

A Cozy Christmas Escape

The Christmas Reunion

The Saltwater Sunsets Series

Whale Harbor Dreams

Whale Harbor Sisters

Whale Harbor Reunions

Whale Harbor Horizons

Whale Harbor Vows

Whale Harbor Blooms

Whale Harbor Adventures

Whale Harbor Blessings

For a full list of my books and series, visit my website at www.fionabakerauthor.com!

ABOUT THE AUTHOR

Fiona writes sweet, feel-good contemporary women's fiction and family sagas with a bit of romance.

She hopes her characters will start to feel like old friends as you follow them on their journeys of love, family, friendship, and new beginnings. Her heartwarming storylines and charming small-town beach settings are a particular favorite of readers.

When she's not writing, she loves eating good meals with friends, trying out new recipes, and finding the perfect glass of wine to pair them with. She lives on the East Coast with her husband and their two trouble-making dogs.

Follow her on her website, Facebook, or Bookbub.

Sign up to receive her newsletter, where you'll get free books, exclusive bonus content, and info on her new releases and sales!